Struggles of A Made Man

II

"The Struggle

Continues"

By: David A.

June 25 2006

Prologue

So we meet again, I hope you were fortunate enough to have read the prequel to this riveting story you're about to experience. This sequel will take you on a journey through the streets of Philly, B-More, Dc, and New York. Will the PDK hustlahs be able to handle the onslaught of D.C. and West Virginia? There's one way to find out, which all begins on the next page...

<P. D. K>

All Day...

Acknowledgments

This is to all the people that supported the first book and have enjoyed it to the fullest. The promo that my mom put out was phenomenal and the praise that I received for the first book I am glad I had the opportunity to share this gift with you all. To make the pot greater I have made this a Trilogy and you will be happy to know it is as good as the first I have the fire and I am using it, although I will try not to get burnt out I know I have loyal readers and the public is who I aim to please as far as the reading goes...☺

"There's been an increase in the murder rate in Philly since the 90's. Last year there was an explosion on the New Jersey turnpike that claimed the lives of four individuals. The investigation was put off due to lack of evidence at the scene..."

"Damn!" Buck said as the news was going off.

"The game is different now, never know who you really dealing with. Seems to be a potential cop on every corner, the way niggas gettin booked."

"Yeah what can you do? That's the risk we have to take to get this money." Smooth said.

"We own damn near half the city so if niggas start talking word will eventually get back to us. All we have to do is lay back and listen."

"Yeah shit has been real smooth for us which I'm happy about. A when Crock say he was coming back?" Smooth asked as he was changing the channel.

"I don't know you'd have to holla at Rell about that."

"When are yall getting off your asses to do something?" Tameka snapped as she was coming down the steps.

"Stop with all that noise, one of the perks of our jobs is we make money while sitting down."

Tameka sat on the couch and said, "Sounds like yall got lazy since Crock disappeared."

"Nah we got a few young niggas movin out right now." Smooth said as he was still flicking through the channels.

"I wonder what he's been up to for almost a year in the south." Buck said walking towards the window.

"I don't know but we need to holla at that nigga "E" from D.C.!" Smooth said as he began to rub his girl's feet.

"Why what's up?" Buck asked turning from the window.

"Remember we had beef about some money a month ago?"

"Oh yeah"

"After that I put them niggas Mil and Streetz up there in B-more to keep an eye open, and build their cred for future references. Cause you never know when we may have to drop him." Smooth said.

"Crock know about that?" Buck asked

"Nah I haven't had time to bring it up to him." Both Buck and Tameka looked at

Smooth like he was joking. Buck broke the silence with

"You know this could bite us in the ass if "E" thinks we tryin him." Buck said as he looked back at the window.

"They got it plus if anything pops off they'll call." Smooth said with confidence.

"Yeah...I hope so!"

"Why you keep looking out the window? What you paranoid?" Tameka said jokingly.

"I aint scared of shit and don't forget that shit!" Buck snapped his head from the window to show he was serious, and continued. "I was wondering who this nigga was down the street with that black nova."

"Where?" Smooth asked getting up from the couch to see, as they looked out the window there were two men both who looked small in stature and they had two other niggas sitting on the nova. Smooth identified one as Prince a youngin he had issues with before, the other three he didn't know. They bumped into this team on a few occasions and thought nothing of them. They were testing the patients of the older more experienced team, even they weren't prepared for what was gonna happen to them in the near future...

"Nah I don't know the two on the car the light skinned dude's name is Prince."

"Aight I'll check their plate when I go past cause I gotta check them niggas Crock put on."

"Who Lil Ron and Fat Cat?"

"Yeah they should be finished by now, Oh yeah "Q" called for another thirty." Buck said.

"Aight I'll go to the spot to get everything together."

"Aight dog, I'll see you and Meka!" Buck said while leaving the crib. As he got in the car he glanced down the street to see the group getting larger. Thinking to himself he wondered who these niggas were to be forming a crowd on the block. "THA GR8 1" was what the plate said and as he drew closer the plate stated they were from D.C. he knew they weren't visiting. He drove past and headed to Jersey to collect from Lil Ron and Fat-Cat...

"Yo what you need?" Mil said to the buyer known as Tank.

"I need fifteen or twenty."

"I got twenty for you but I need to see the money first." When he finished he pulled his cell and waited to hear Tanks response.

"Aight!" he said and looked back at his dark SUV. The door opened and out stepped a short Asian chick with long black hair. She had a silver briefcase hand cuffed to her waist. She walked over with the elegance of a model and her body was curvy for an Asian. She held the case out and tank opened it revealing 6 rows of 60 thousand.

"Aight" Mil said as he checked the bills. "It's all good, hold up." he said then dialed a number and waited for an answer.

"Yo"

"A Streetz bring twenty up for me."

"Aight here I come." As Mil finished the call he looked at his watch.

"Everything copastetic?" Tank asked.

"Yeah he's coming now with it."

Tank uncuffed the briefcase and handed it to Mil. After taking the case a grey celebrity rolled up and Streetz stepped out.

"Here go your work cuz."

Once again Tank gestured to the SUV and another Asian broad came out. They both grabbed the gym bags from Streetz and went back to the car.

"I hope to do business with you again sometime." Tank said as he got into the wheel and rolled out.

"A what up cuz?" Streetz asked

"Aint shit tryin to handle this B.I... here take this back to the crib for me."

"A you hear that nigga "E" mad cause his shit aint movin like it was."

"So fuck that nigga! He good as dead anyway fuckin with P.D.K." Mil responded.

"You right! Look I gotta holla at this pretty young thing in downtown B-more. Just call me if you need. Streetz said as he was getting in the car.

"Aight fam, I need to relax anyway. I might go to a bar or a club." As their conversation ended Mil got into his LS 400 and rolled down the ship...

"A Ron!" yelled Buck. "Come here right quick."

Ron knew he was short a couple hundred so he took it from his own stash to make it right. It's obvious Fat-Cat was trimming him. He strolled over to Buck and extended his fist for a dap.

"What up my nigga?" showing respect.

"Aint shit, look you got that for me?" Buck said getting right to the point.

"Yeah" handing him a wad of cash, ruffling through the bills Buck was satisfied it was all there. He gave Ron a bag and told him.

"Be sure to keep in touch. Oh! Watch out for SUV's with VA. Plates. And where that nigga Fat-Cat?"

"He probably at the spot, you hear from Crock yet?"

"What you worried about him for?" Buck snapped.

"He told me to let him know if we have any problems with another strip. These niggas reppin D.C. hard screamin Dip set and shit"

"Dip set! Aight I'll let him know."

"A let him know they suppose to be movin for some nigga named "E" out D.C."

"How you know?" Buck asked.

"You'd be surprised what bitches know when the money comes out."

"Aight lil nigga you on point, holla if you hear anything else." Buck drove off and paged Crock to hit his cell. Then went to Italiano's to grab some food for him and Jas...

Chapter 2

"Aight ma good look on the picture."
"No problem, just be sure to tell your friends about us."
"Aight." Rell said as he made his way past the grand opening banners. Once outside Rell glanced at there name,
<The Nubian Experience>
He felt excited about the picture he picked out for Mel's crib. It had a black man and woman tied in each others arms with a couple black jaguars on either side of them. They were in a position that resembled that of the Karma Sutra. Both sitting on a Golden Fleece rug with the sun sitting behind them which made a very exquisite hue across the sky. Rell just knew she would fall in love with it. Although it cost $37 dollars it would be worth it in the stretch. He already grabbed the money from his man "J". James was Rell and Crocks man for years then he got booked a little more than a

year before Crock and Rell. When he came home about a month ago Rell put him on so he could get on his feet. About ten minutes from the crib Rell called Mel.

"Hello" she answered with her soft voice.

"What's up boo?"

"Aint nothin waiting for you to come home. You do know this is my day off right?"

"Of course I do. I had to handle a little bit of business and I called to see if you wanted anything to eat?"

"Yeah, but you can't buy what I need to be served."

"Look at you talking all crazy, and you say you're a church girl.' Rell said jokingly.

"Look you playin I just want you home."

"Aight I'll be there in a couple minutes. Oh I got a surprise for you too."

"I'll be waiting…"

It was blazin hot on the beach; I was just chillin outside my new lil condo that was on the beach. These chicks be walkin around all day and all night with thong bikinis on. Man that shit is intoxicating. A nigga could get into some shit if he wasn't careful. You know bitches aint

shit, they'll set a nigga up in a
heartbeat... Some get pregnant on a nigga
to trap him.
"Could you buy me a drink?" a voice
asked from behind me with a sexy little
accent. Without looking I said;
"It all depends on your intentions after
the drinks."
"That all depends on the drinks bought."
She said with a hint of seduction. I
turned to see pure beauty. She stood no
taller than five foot,
Curves were devilish. She had green eyes
which stood out as did her pretty feet.
After seeing her I wanted a little more
than just drinks. She had the accent of a
Roslyn Sanchez and the body of a Stacey
Dash.
"So, about that drink?" She asked again.
"Yeah about that drink. Look I got some
shit in the crib if you wanna chill a bit."
"How far is it?" She asked looking up and
down the beach.
"Right there," I said as I pointed to it. I
was wondering if she was one of them
gold diggahs. She looked at the crib and
said,
"Okay I see you got your shit together.

Aint that many men with there shit tight
out here. Those that do are either
smugglers or slingers."
"I just bought this crib and came down
from Philly to chill." I got up and picked
up my towels and started to the house. I
walked slowly so I could admire go gods
perfection. All in all I wanted to hit. When
we got to the crib I dusted the sand off
the towels and told her where the bar
was.
"You're in luck." She said with a bit of a
smirk.
"I know, Ever since I entered your
presence." She smiled and said,
"You funny, I was talking about being a
bartender." I couldn't help but watch how
her body moved around the kitchen. She
looked back at me to see my reaction.
"A bartender huh? Where at?"
"A little spot on the strip called Latoya's
Bar and Grill." Handing me a drink she
mixed up she continued with,
"You should come through sooner than
later. I'm real good with my hands." She
walked over and started to rub my
shoulders.
"Damn that feels good; I may take you up

on that offer. So, what up with you? I'm
pretty sure you gotta man."
"Nah, I'm alone out here. I got a place
about ten minutes from the beach." I
stood and turned around and backed her
up to the sink. Standing chest to chest I
leaned in and whispered in her ear.
"Would you like to see the rest of the
house?" her response shocked me
because it was like she was reading my
mind.
"I'd just much rather see your bedroom.
I'm sure there's something we both would
like to get off our chests."
"Say no more." I said as I grabbed her
hand and took her straight to the room.
As Soon as we went into the room, she
threw me onto the bed and climbed on
top of me. Being as though I had my
shorts on and she had a thong bikini
there wasn't much to remove. Yet she
made it feel like days went by. She licked
on my chest and bit on my ear lobes.
Then she started back down my chest to
my navel. Then she took my shorts off
and began to suck on my dick with such
delicacy that the warmth alone had me
ready to cum. She untied her top with my

dick still in her mouth. She was going like she aint wanna stop. Then she stood and took off her bottom and sat astride my dick, and began to buck her hips back and forth. I caressed her nipples as she started moaning. Her pace picked up and she leaned forward and put most of her weight on my shoulders and she lost it. Screaming she was Cumming and then she seized up, I could feel her vaginal walls constrict around my dick which brought me to my own climax. She fell onto my chest and asked me to hold her in my arms, so I did just that. It was intense but she had me at hello. I mean a nigga didn't wanna go back to Philly, feeling the sandman at the back of my eyelids I slowly dosed off with her in my arms asshole naked...

Smooth finished his food and thought of that nigga "E" may act up if he realizes Mil and Streetz are out there to eventually drop him. Word is he tight with some niggas from Wes V.
"You like your food honey?" Tameka asked as she filled his cup with more orange juice.
"Yeah bay, this shit slammin as usual."

"You want some more?"

"Nah I gotta go handle something right quick." He said as he downed his juice.

"Aight, well it's more in there if you want." She told him as she left the kitchen to the living room. Smooth finished cleaning his dishes and left for the spot. In the car he noticed them same niggas were still with the boy Prince. Smooth slowed and signaled him over.

"Yo what you looking for?" he asked

"Nigga do I look like I use? Who the fuck you out here for?" Smooth asked with a strong tone in his voice.

"Who you to be concerned?!" the light skinned nigga spat back. Smooth already anticipated their reaction so he had his burner in his hand just in case.

"Look I'm telling you young niggas once, this aint yall corner to be hustling on. Don't be here tonight, oh and tell your boss P.D.K. run this shit here!" with that said Smooth sped off. He went to the spot and got thirty bricks together for the journey to N.Y. he hollered at James and found out that Rell left about an hour ago. Smooth let James know that he would need him to ride with him tonight.

"There were some young niggas who need a lesson in this game." He said. When he got everything stashed he called "Q".

"Yo" he answered "Your timing is a little fucked up." he said while trying to handle his business with another bad bitch he met at the garden.

"Hang up the phone Quincy I need you to slap it. How you gonna do that with your hands on the phone?" she asked in the background.

"My bad "Q" I was calling to let you know I'm on my way with your kids." Smooth said.

"Aight son holla when you get to the spot."

"Aight."

Smooth knows Crock told him never to deliver anything anywhere with out some one to watch your back. Especially out of state. It looked like everyone was busy so he called "J" and asked.

"Yo that nigga Titus in there?"

"I don't know I last saw him by the steps of the abandon crib."

Titus was a thorough nigga that was that was riding with us through our bid. Smooth went into the crib and saw Titus sitting at a table with D-nice, Tone, and Ant playing spades.

"Yo Titus come take this ride with me!"

"Aight here I come." Titus stood with his tall slender frame and put his guns in his holsters and grabbed his coat.

"Where we heading" he asked as they were leaving.

"To N.Y. if any one needs me my new cell # in the car is (267) 253-2397."

"Aight they said simultaneously

Smooth and Titus made their way to the car door and Smooth asked.

"Yo I may be calling you to come through if not I will holla at you in the a.m."

"Aight" they both got in and started on their two hour road trip...

Chapter 3

Mil has been riding around for a minute and finally found a nice little spot called Ecstasy. There was a small line forming at the door. Mil parked and went straight to the front to holla at the bouncer, knowing he had his nine Millie on him he still tried to go in.

"Yo my man you can't just walk in." he

said extending his arm to slow and stop him. Mil figured everyone has his price. "Listen here my man there's two things wrong with this picture. I don't listen to anyone but me and my team don't like lines."

"Well I'm sorry you'll have to wait the place is full as of now." Mil went into his pocket and pulled out one of his smaller knots. He started to peel off three hundred but decided two will be good then said,

"I think there's room for one more, don't you?" He said as he palmed the money to the bouncer through a hand shake.

"As a matter of fact there is enough for just one more." The bouncer stepped to the side, as Mil walked in he could see the place was definitely jumping from wall to wall. Mil was in the mood to relax so he went to the bar to have a few drinks. Listening to the mix of Fifty Cent and Pac while niggas were going crazy. Then someone grabbed him on his shoulder. Mils first instinct was to pull his gun and shoot but he looked first.

"Are you the one who tipped my bouncer?" The well dressed man asked.

"It may be a possibility, who's asking?"
Mil asked with his hand on his gun still.
"My name is Harry and this is one of my
clubs. I also own club Parish down the
strip.
"Okay I see! So what you need with me?"
Mil asked as he eased up a little and
sipped his Gin and Tonic.
"I figure we could go to the V.I.P. lounge
and have a couple, if you're up to it?" He
asked as he pointed to the room above
the club.
"Yeah if there's some fine ass bitches up
there too."
"Of course there are. I have women that
only work the V.I.P. and the rest are
down here." As they made their way
through the crowd they went through a
door that led to some stairs up. At the top
the lounge was quiet and luxurious.
Three chicks ran up to Mil and Harry as
soon as they sat down. Mil was pleased to
see that the women up here were all
dimes. Not a scratch, scar, or blemish
that could be seen. And they didn't leave
much to the imagination with G-strings
and thongs. The ladies began to put on a
show for them and Mil felt the pills he

popped begin to take effect. After a while the ladies began to give Mil a lap dance.
"Looks like you're enjoying yourself." Harry said sipping his Pina Colada Grey Goose.
"Yeeaahh" Mil Slurred.
"You like her don't you? We all love Carmen. She Good."

She leaned in while on Mils lap and nibbled on his ear and whispered,
"If you really feelin me like I feel your dick, I get off at two o'clock." Mil knew she could feel him but the drinks and the pills got him bent and lazy. He whispered back,
"I'll be here cause a nigga need to relax and you definitely helping with that."
"So young brotha what's your name?" Harry asked.
"My homies call me Mil and my enemies call me nothing at all."
"Why's that?"
"Cause when I deal with them they have no face to speak from." He said as he laid his head back.
"I feel you, can I ask you something?" he said as he got serious.
"It depends on what it is!"

"I'm looking to buy some keys but I don't know where to go. You see my supplier has been on a drought or beef with that bitch Tori from Wes. V Cause that's where he was movin from."

"How you figure I'd know anything about some drugs?"

"My bouncer seen you rollin with a couple of those P.D.K. niggas a week ago.

"Your bouncer seems to know a lot.' Mil said as he began to feel uneasy about him.

"I need him to know a lot because he's my body guard. I've been at war with these D.C niggas for about a year now. See I got niggas where most wouldn't look." Mil glanced around and couldn't find anything.

"It's like that huh?" he asked.

"Man them D.C. pussies try to creep inside the club and we throw them out the back in trash bags."

"I'll look into that for you, but who you at war with in D.C?" mil asked.

"You may have heard of him he go by "E" to most but I know him as Erin."

"Damn. Look I'll get at you about that other thing but a nigga need to chill right now!" Mil laid his head back and Carmen laid back on him and grabbed his hands and caressed her tits with them.

"Well I will give you this for future references. She said writing something down "hope to hear from you" handing him the paper. Mil just relaxed and enjoyed the dance...

Knock, Knock, Knock. Streetz knocked at the door of a muse he met about a week ago. She was half black and half Asian with a Phat ass and a bow in her legs. What really caught his eye wasn't her big breasts or her pretty feet. It was how straight forward she was. She liked to get to the point.

"Hello" she said sounding as sexy as she did when they first met.

"It's me Streetz" he answered trying to imagine what she had on behind the door. The lock clicked and the door opened. She stood there in a pair of silk boxers and a very big T-shirt.

"Damn Trinity" he said as he walked in to give her a hug. She sexy even I a shirt and boxers, he thought to himself.

"You want something to eat?" she asked as they walked in the kitchen. Streetz grabbed her by the hand and pulled her close and said.

"I'm hungry for something other than food right now!" as he started to nibble on her ear lobe. She cooed a little trying to resist the urge, but caved to his advances. She slid out of the boxers and jumped on the counter. Streetz unceremoniously slipped his pants off and began to steer his weapon to her love box but stopped.

"What's wrong?" she asked.

"Nah, Nothin. You got a condom?" thinking she could be a trick. Without movin she opened the drawer and pulled one out. Once he slipped it on he started to fuck her on the counter. Her pussy was so hot that he couldn't feel the condom. Not only was it hot it was tight as her body. He continued to drill her until she started scratching his back out of pleasure.

"I want you to fuck me from behind." She moaned and hopped down. She led him to the arm of the sofa where she laid across it. He continued to stroke her for another five minutes and felt himself about to cum but was so deep in his stroke that he couldn't pull out or didn't want to. She also was reaching her peak and they met their climaxes together. When he was finished he went to the bathroom where he flushed the condom. He turned and got the shower on and took off his shirt. Trinity walked over and asked.

"Is there enough room for one more?"

"You know it is." He replied. They began washing each other and talking about the next time they meet what kind of things they would do to each other...

Chapter 4

Buck and Jas were finished their food and were watching a movie on Cinimax. Buck still hadn't heard from Crock and thought it was necessary he knew about them D.C. niggas teamin up with the Dipset. Grabbing his phone he called Crock on his cell.

"Hello"

"Crock you up?" Buck asked.

"I am now, why what's up?" sounding groggy.

"Yo that nigga "E" teamed up with some of those Dipset niggas!" Sitting up I was wide awake now.

"Yeah! When you hear this?"

"Earlier today. I tried to page you but never heard back from you."

"Keep your eyes open and ears to the street and let me know if any thing else comes up."

"Good morning big boy" the woman's voice said in the background.

"Hold up for a minute I'm on the phone." I said trying to silence her.

"Damn who that?" Buck asked.

"Latoya. She own this little bar up here and she insisted that we get to know each other! Look we got the whole tri-state on lock. If them niggas step outta line take initiative and handle it!"

"Aight Crock, look when you comin back?"

"Maybe in a couple days, cause we may have to move on "E" or one of his sets to let him know he can be touched.

"Aight I'll call if anything comes up."

"Aight" Buck hung up the phone and continued to watch the movie, and then his phone rang again.

"Yo"

"Buck them niggas that were on the corner have til tonight to leave or we'll make the corner their permanent residence." Smooth said with a serious tone.

"You call the boys or we movin alone?"

"There were three when I left. Oh did you hear from Rell today?"

"Nah"

"I did call him but aint get through. Oh I told Ant to come through later."

"Think we should call Rell again?" Buck asked.

"I'll try to call him again."

"What time we going down there?"

"Like ten thirty."

"Aight I'll be there in an hour..."

Ron walked over to his man and shoved him.

"Cat, a Fat-Cat" Fat-Cat has been lazy recently and his slacking is costing money.

"Yo take your ass home if you gonna sleep nigga!" Ron spat at him.

"I'm up, I'm up"

"Nah nigga you can't do shit but be in my fuckin way so go home."

"Aight I'm going." Fat-Cat got up and made his way to the door. He disappeared from site and Ron continued stashing the money and locked up. He left feeling that he had to cut that nigga off cause he gonna get someone killed. He too fuckin lazy and he never on point. He hated to think the one he got killed would be him. The thoughts were unnerving so he went home to take a bath...

Walking into the crib Fat-Cat threw his jacket on the floor and yelled for his woman.

"Jenny?! A Jenny!?" he called. Jenny was a psycho before meeting Fat-Cat. There was something in him that changed her or did it?

"I'm in the kitchen." she said.

"You make me somethin to eat?"

"I thought you had eaten since you been out so late."

"Damn! You stupid bitch you know I be hungry."

"I got your bitch, keep that shit up" she said as she became angry.

"You aint doin shit!"

Jenny knew how he always liked to come in and drink milk. This time she chose to slip him a micky, and watch as he downed the last of it.

"Maybe, just maybe you could do something right for a change and please your man!" he slurred at her. She complied and followed him to he bedroom. He flopped on the bed and slipped his pants and shirt off. Jenny liked to think she had a good head game, so she climbed up and slurped him into her mouth. She had to work with him a while to get him erect. Once he was she swallowed his whole man and made good work of it. She figured it may be the last one he gets. After a while of sucking his sweaty man he nutted in her mouth. She still slurped every drop of him, it was her nature. She looked up at him as she was wiping her mouth on the sheets, and seen the drug was taking effect. He looked to be fighting the sleep but was losing. She got up and went into the kitchen and pulled out a big pot and filled it with water then cut on the stove. Once the water began to boil she rummaged through the cabinet and found some Mrs. Butterworth and poured the whole bottle in the pot. Thinking this is worse than the time she crazy glued Alex's dick to his leg and his fingers and toes together in his sleep.

"Yeah this shit gonna stick to yo ass." She said aloud.

"This is for all those times you hit me and cheated on me. Here go your BITCH! BITCH!"

She grabbed the pot covers and carried the boiling hot mixture into the bed room. Watching his sleeping state she convinced herself to throw the liquid lava on him. He screamed louder than anything she ever heard. It was so loud she dropped the pot and covered her ears. The pain looked unbearable; his skin looked to peel from the bone when he stood. It looked so disgusting she ran from the room and locked herself in the bathroom. After a couple minutes the squeals stopped, she came out to see him stretched out on his bedroom floor. She grabbed her things and left the house...

"Ringgg, Ringgg" the phone rang "Hello" Rell answered with a yawn.

"Yo it's Smooth you up? I hope so cause we gotta lay some heat on these young niggas up the end."

Damn when?" Rell asked wiping the coal from his eyes.

"In about twenty minutes we gonna meet up at the spot and roll from there."

"Aight I'm there!" Rell finished the call and slipped out of bed without waking Mel. He went into the bathroom and washed his face and brushed his teeth. When he was finished he went to the bedroom and grabbed his guns off the bed post. He grabbed a box of bullets from the closet and started loading his clips in the living room. When he was finished he left for the meet. On the way he hyped himself up with some D.M.X. "X is coming". Turning on to 17th street he could see that Buck, Smooth, and Ant were already here, by their cars. He parked and went into the spot to find everyone was sitting and waiting on him.

"Aight we all here now!" Smooth said

"So lets get down to it" there's only one way into the strip so we can split up and have two and two."

"What about the crossfire?" Buck asked.

"Couldn't we just send somebody they don't know to see if they're out there?" Ant said making sense.

"Look fuck all the bullshittin around. These niggas may not even be strapped. I'm going down there and I'm not gonna plan some shit out for a bunch of flunkies." Rell said.

"I'm with him" replied Buck.

"Shit! I got my vest and both my 45's are loaded." Rell said and turned towards the door. Buck got up and followed him out.

"I guess we ridin out" Smooth said seeing it was him and Ant last to leave the crib. When Buck and Rell rolled down the block Buck pointed the young niggas Nova out on the corner. Rell stopped and walked up to the dice game on the corner. They couldn't see Smooth and Ant posted up on the wall behind them. Seeing Buck jump out of the car three tried to run but ran into a hail of bullets from Smooth and Ant. The others stood in dismay knowing they slipped.

"Move and you're dead! Blink and you're dead! Breath and you're dead, you got me?" Rell hissed with both his hammers out. Knowing there's always one who needs to be made an example of, and then it happened.

"I got you old head w..." he was met with

two shots in the face.

"I thought I was clear apparently he didn't understand the move Blink, Breath and you're dead! A didn't my man tell you this our corner?" Rell asked as Buck chimed in with

"Yall niggas screamin that Dipset shit well we bout to Dip yall whole Set!" there was a crack of a hammer cocking. The streets have never been this quiet. Rell moved one of them from the group and gave Buck, Ant and Smooth the signal. Then bullets started screamin and bodies started bleedin. When the silence of death echoed in the streets again Rell asked.

"I'ma ask you something if I feel as though you lying I'ma slay you." He nodded in compliance.

"Who you working for lil nigga?"

"This nigga from D.C. put us to work about a week ago."

"Yall just sellin or yall lookouts?" Rell asked.

"Both, we watchin some P.D.K. niggas. He claim he gonna drop them soon. That's all I know.

"You know" Rell said as he used one of the hammers to scratch his head like he

was thinking and continued.
"The crazy part about all this I really believe you"
BOOM!!!
Rell shot him in the chest. He crumbled and asked "why you shoot me? I thought you believed me."
"No reason" **BOOM! BOOM! BOOM! BOOM!** Another day ends with blood spilled and lives wasted...

Chapter 5

After receiving the phone call I could sleep. Plus there was a bad little chick in the bed next to me. I'll call Rell tomorrow to see if he heard anything like that. Cause if "E" teamed with them "Piss-Pets" we could holla at "Q" and Tank from B-More. Them niggas from D.C. aint that big, but no one knows how deep the Piss-Pets are. With that said I decided to holla at Stretch later on. I'll ask if he's heard anything new about them niggas. Damn I haven't seen Meme in a while I know she gonna snap at me. I got up and jumped in the shower after I brushed my teeth. I continued to think of Meme and how she always been in my corner. There aint no reason to be so distant with her, I know she been feelin me and my feelings are the same. I just don't wanna involve her in this type of life. As I got out I dried off and I could smell some food. I slipped into my boxers and shorts and went into the kitchen. In front of the stove with one of my robes stood Latoya throwing down.

"Good morning Lala" I said as I walked up behind her and kissed her on her neck and nibbled on her ear.

"I like that"

"What the kiss or last night?" I asked

"All three" she said as she was messin around with the pan.

"All three what are you talkin about?"

"The kiss and the name Lala. I'm used to being called Toya and of course last night. I can't remember the last time I hit three orgasms."

"Bullshit! You had one I know of cause I still got the marks to prove it. I don't know where the other two came from."

"You stupid"

"How? You sure they were with me or did you have a wand in your purse?" laughing she said

"You crazy, try this" picking up a piece of food.
"What's this?"
"Apiece of omelet."
      I ate it and really couldn't believe she could really hold hers in the kitchen. That shit was slammin.
"Damn Ma that was good!"
"I hoped you'd like it. I don't usually cook for any one."
"Not even for your brothers or sisters?"
"I was an only child and my mom was stingy with the kitchen."
Ha, that's crazy; oh I gotta go to Philly to handle something."
"Will I see you again?" looking concerned.
"I hate promises Ma but I will try to see you again. But you aint gotta go you can stay till you want to leave."
""When today?"
"Nah when ever. That way you don't have to be so far from work."
"Are you serious?"
"I feel as though I can trust you. I wouldn't wanna feel as though I've been crossed cause then people would surly get hurt."
"Aint nobody trying to cross you. I'm just

shocked you would trust me with your crib."

"Yeah, yeah. I'm barely hear and I'll know it was lived in. so you gonna stay or leave?" I said

"I'll stay. So when you leaving?"

"Probably tomorrow."

'Tomorrow! Damn you at least have to come check out my spot on the strip."

"Aight let me get dressed first."

'Hurry up too!" she said as she got into some close of mine...

A few hours passed and Mil was ready to go, knowing he was high he called Rell to tell him the news on "E" before he forgot. Grabbing his cell he dialed the number.

"Yo" Rell answered

"A Rell it's Mil, I got some news for you and Crock. I didn't wanna forget so I called you."

"What's up homie?" asked Rell

"I'm in B-More at some club called Ecstasy
and the owners heard of us. He looking to buy some shares. I played dumb cause I don't know this nigga."

"That's it?"

"Nah this nigga said he claim to be at war with this nigga named Erin or "E.""
"For real? Damn, that nigga tryin to pull some fast shit down here. See if you can find anything else out and holla back."
"Aight" hanging up Mil made his way to the lounge and was halfway to the door when he heard a voice call.
"You leaving so soon? I'm off in about five minutes." Turning he said
"Yeah I'll pick up things with you later, a nigga been up too late."
"Aight can a girl get your number?" pulling out a pen Mil jotted his digits onto a napkin.
"Don't lose that cause I may not be around here for a couple of days.
"Aight I'll call you tomorrow sometime."
"Aight" he said as he turned back towards the door. On his way out he gave the bouncer a nod. He jumped in the car and rolled to his apartment...
"It must be over he left a year ago and didn't tell me he was leaving." Meme said crying.
"He probably had to handle something, you know that boy all about that money." Mel said to calm her girl nerves. She

Meme and Tameka were all sprawled out on the living room floor at Memes' crib. The television was on but muted and they had snacks and drinks on the coffee table.

It was another one of their girl's night out, but they've been talking about Memes' boyfriends disappearing act for the past two weeks. Mel didn't know what she could say to calm her spirits. She's been broken hearted since she found out that he left.

"What happened to make him leave?"

"I don't know I got up one day and he wasn't home."

"Were you at his house?"

"Yeah he was there when I went to sleep. I got up the next day and everyone was asking where he was."

"Did you call him?" Tameka kept asking her questions.

"Yeah he left a message saying things got intense and he had to leave and then it stopped." Meme said as she started to wipe her eyes.

"Intense the hell that suppose to mean?" asked Meka.

"Maybe he wasn't happy with me or I was

moving too fast and I scared him off."
"I don't know girl I barely know him but he didn't come off as that type of dude. He looked to me like he handled his shit." Meka said as she grabbed a soda off the table.
"Yeah girl he's one of the few that may put his girl first or at least make her feel first. Plus I never seen him with anyone else." Melanie said as she was finishing up Meme's hair. She put corn rows in, something she could be doing professionally but never went for a license.
"Did you try to call him back?" Meka asked
"I tried a couple times but the phone was out of range or something."
"Girl don't worry there's someone out there for you. Don't worry yourself, you got more important things to worry about than a no good worthless nigga." Tameka said not realizing how devoted Meme was to Crock. Meme snapped.
"Bitch! Don't be talking shit; he's a good fuckin man. He helped your man and his family through their rough times. He loves me and you better realize that

before you slander him again." Memes eyes were still filled with pain but she did feel a little better, now that she vented a little steam.

"Yall need to calm down. Crock will call or show up when he handles his shit. You don't even know if he left to protect you. He's like that, but first thing you need to do is relax."

Melanie said as she stood and stretched, then said

"Yall my girls and we all need to just relax." Turning on the volume and they all began to watch the movie...

"Come on Tommy. I'm only short a couple. Give me a break." The fiend begged knowing he may not see tomorrow.

"Naw dog you out your mind. You know what I do to niggas who short!" knowing where he was getting at the fiend pushed Tommy and broke out. Tommy gave chase but couldn't keep up.

"No wonder niggas call me slow. I can't even catch a fiend." He said to himself he pulled out his P89 and bussed four shots at him. One hit the fiend in the back and dropped him. Tommy immediately looked around and ran up on him.

"You aint so fast now are you?" Tommy asked as he took aim at the fiends face. Yelling the fiend said, "Come on blood you aint gotta do this." Coughing up blood over Tommy's shoes. Pissed Tommy snapped and unloaded the remainder of the clip into the fiend.

"I just bought these fuckin sneaks." Tommy said as he went into the pockets of the lifeless body. Feeling a little disgusted Tommy went to the Duckie spot to chill and clean his sneaks...

Ring, Ring, Ring,

"Hello"

"Yo you see the news nigga?"

"Nah why?" Ron asked

"Cause your man dead!" the voice said.

"Stop playin who the fuck is this?" he snapped

"It's Titus I've been watching the news and they said he was so severely burned that he probably died within five minutes of the initial contact with the mixture."

"Damn, they say how he did it?"

"They aint say he did it. They think it was thrown on him cause they found large traces of syrup on his flesh and sheets.

You know his girl right?"

"Yeah she probably already know. I'll call to see if she heard." Ron said.

"Aight dog I talked to Rell earlier and he got me and D-nice and Dame coming up to hold it down with you"

"Aight I gotta holla at him anyway."

As he hung up he noticed his bed was empty. Miranda must have been at work cause the place was quiet.

He got out of bed and went to handle his hygiene. While in the shower he couldn't help but think of how his man got burned. That shit just sounded backwards. Then he thought of Fat Cats girl. She aint all there herself. But to kill someone she allegedly loved. "Man that bitch crazy, I don't even wanna say shit to her crazy ass." He was saying to himself. Drying off he went into the bedroom and got dressed. He was wondering if them niggas from D.C. were making a move. He felt he had to do something about them niggas. Walking through the kitchen he grabbed his keys and left the crib. He went to the spot and grabbed some work. Even thought the block was dead except the usuals who are always out this early.

"What you need?" he asked his first customer.

"That good get you up! He handed Ron a fifty and Ron gave him a small package and left then the next man came up and this process went on for the rest of the morning...

Chapter 6

Streetz was sitting in his car outside Mils crib honking the horn. Feeling he must still be sleep he got out of the car and went to the door and knocked.

"A Mil get your ass up! There's money to be made." Hearing no response he turned the handle and seen it was opened. So he went in, soon as the door opened he understood why he couldn't hear him. The stereo was on and it seemed to be fairly warm in the crib. Streetz turned the radio down and heard the shower on.

"A Mil" he yelled

"Yo what's up?"

"Come on man we got shit to do today."

He heard the shower shut off and the radio was down so he felt he could stop yelling.

"Didn't you hear from Crock or Rell yet?"

"Nah why?" Mil asked.

"Cause this shit is vicious. I wanna start making some major money."

"I do too. You know these niggas out here aint all on point. We could watch one of their strips and drop a nigga." Mil was saying as he laced up his Nikes.

"We can roll around and see what these niggas are up to."

"Aight lets roll."

They both left the crib and started to roll around B-more for a minute, then went to D.C. to see where niggas are movin out there. They found some young nigga that looked new in the game. Mil pulled the car over and they watched the young boa for the rest of the afternoon...

Across town a young nigga named Tone who got out about eight months ago has been movin out for Crock while in the county. Tone was chillin with his man on the corner of 23rd and Indiana, when he seen a couple cars rollin down the block. This the third time he seen the black SUVs. Buck put them onto them outta state niggas and how they tryin to take over. The plates were West Virginian; they both went into the crib and watched the vehicles roll by again. They new this was the work of an ambush. They immediately called Rell.

'Yo what's up?"

"Rell its Tone and Cash. We seen these niggas from West V. again. This the third time this afternoon what should we do?"

"Yo be cool we be down there soon. How long ago they leave?"

"They just turned the corner." Tone said as he looked out the window.

"Aight, think yall could follow them?"

"Yeah that's what Cash is known for."

"Aight handle that then get back to me. I'ma holla at Buck and the boys."

"Aight" he hung up and stood up on the couch Cash looked at him.

"What's up?" he asked

"We gotta follow these niggas. Rell getting the team together."

"What we gonna move on them niggas today?" Cash asked as they rushed to get into the car.

"I think Buck said they were movin all over, they in D.C. and B-more."

"Damn I heard some niggas called Dipset

movin out too."

"Yeah but they not knockin niggas off like these West V. niggas."

"Oh"

They followed them at a safe distance and made sure not to be seen at the lights too. They went all the way down East Falls into some Duplex type building. They waited a little less than a block away to see if they were coming back out. After a half went pass Tone called Rell back.

"Yo what's up youngin?"

"They pulled into a duplex down East falls. It aint far from Montgomery. They aint come out yet, I think this is they spot. Its crazy cause the place got torn down buildings on both sides of it. They just sittin in there now though."

"Aight let me finish roundin everyone up! A don't move unless they move you get me?" Rell asked rhetorically

"Yeah we got you. He hung up and told Cash the news. One person came out and walked down the street. Tone said

"A call Rell if they leave cause I'ma follow this nigga. He may be up to something."

"Aight nigga be safe!" Cash said as Tone

was exiting the car.

"I will."

Tone followed his mark at a safe distance around the block. He wasn't going anywhere far from the looks of it. He went into a local grocery store called "Johns goods." The place looked beat down but so did the rest of the neighborhood. Tone walked into the store and seen that nigga buying sandwiches and sodas so Tone figured they'll be a while. Tone left back to the car and told Cash he bought sandwiches.

"They'll be here for a while."

"Aight" they sat watching until told otherwise...

     The plane landed and I got out with my little luggage. You see I planned on being chewed out so I brought a few gifts and trinkets. I know this don't mean shit cause Meme's always been there for me and not the material things. I don't know why she left that message on my cell. Saying that she meant to tell me something before I disappeared, then said she's got a big surprise for me. I love surprises, but what scares me is Meme hates surprises, so why would she have one for me. Damn I forgot to call Rell, getting into my cab I called him.

"Yo I told yall to relax till we got there!"

"The fuck you talkin about nigga?" confused

"Crock? Crock that's you?"

"Yeah it's me. I see shits been real busy for you out here."

"Like you wouldn't believe, look let me holla at you later on cause Cash and Tone found some of them West V. pussies. I'm tryin to get the team together to make them permanent residents of Philly." Rell said.

"Aight you need me?" I asked happy to hear my man holdin shit down.

"Nah nigga your girl need you. She think you left her or something. "

"She do? Why would she have a surprise for me then?"

"Surprise? Yeah it's different to be a part of something you can't control huh?" Rell said.

"What's that suppose to mean?"

"Look I gotta go Crock, holla at me later."

"Aight"

Hanging up the phone I was wondering what in the hell Rell was talking about!

Shits been busy" I said to myself. "Niggas
from D.C. and West V. been trying our
chins. I gotta be sure to tell the new
recruits cause they may not know how to
handle them. Reese and Twan down from
Frankford ave. don't know about these
niggas. Picking my cell back up I called
them.
"Yo what it be?"
"A Reese, it's me Crock. Yo if you see
some cars ridin around with West V. or
D.C. plates watch yourself. We officially
going to war with these niggas." I said
"Aight I got you. Oh yeah I got that for
you plus my young boa Sid wanna ride
with the team."
"If he do some dumb shit you know it's
on your head." I said sternly, making
sure he understood.
"I know I'll be on top of him. Good lookin
on the heads up."
As I finished the call the taxi pulled up to
the crib. I gave him a buck twenty five
even though the fare was seventy five
dollars from the airport. Walking into the
crib I seen the place wasn't lived in,
which means Meme stayed at home or at
her girls spot. She probably angry with

me still. I told her I was coming home today. Fuck it I got ready for a bath and locked up the house...

Sitting in Rells crib the semi-congregation were discussing their plans before moving on the foreigners. In attendance was Rell, Buck, Smooth, Ant, and James. The plan was to secure the front and have James, Cash and Tone hit the back. Then flood the place at once. Tone and James will stay back and cover Cash as he goes in and dips in the kitchen. When everyone was in compliance they rolled out in two cars...

Chapter 7

Shit began to pick up a little with noon coming to an end. Ron was doing his best to accommodate all the fiends. He noted a blue Civic pulling up. He could tell that it was Titus from his hat. Then a green Blazer pulled up and parked behind Titus, and a Jetta behind his truck, knowing it was them he continued to serve his impatient customers. They all got out and walked up to him.

"You aight out here?" Titus asked

"Naw I could use some help shit getting busy."

"Aight where the stash?" Ron leaned in and whispered where it was in the crib.

"What you need us to do?" D-nice asked

"Help Black count that money. Oh damn keep look out on the roof for some funny shit cause niggas is creepin. Them D.C. niggas and West V. niggas are knockin niggas off."

"Aight"

Titus came back out and started selling. Ron took this opportunity to go re-up and give Black the money. He still was feeling uneasy about his man getting offed. He did his best to keep it the back of his mind so it wouldn't distract him in the streets.

"A Black?" Ron called as he walked up to the table.

"What's up?"

"Can you count this and put it up for me?"

"I got you."

Ron handed him an abnormally large knot and left after he stocked Buck up on his product. After a couple of sales he decided to help Black count and ask

D-nice if he'd finish up out here.

"A "D"? Could you go out for a while cause a nigga is a little exhausted today."

"It aint about shit I go you." He said as he put a stack of money down, then went to grab product. Still counting the money about an hour went by when Dame started yellin.

"A yo?! Some niggas rollin down the block in two black SUVs."

D-nice was already through the door when the bullets began to whistle through the air. They were poppin them semi-autos like it was a Scar face audition. Titus tried to dip behind a car but was stood up with a shot to the ass, and then he was just riddled with bullets from the waist up. Black, Ron, and D-nice were bustin through there self made peep holes through the boarded up windows. Dame was able to hit two from the roof before being hit twice in the stomach which made him tumble off the roof like an old western. Black left and ran around back then shimmied to the side of the crib. Black started bussin and hit one of the drivers in the neck; he tried to hit the other one but the vehicles sped off down the block. Rushing back into the crib Black helped bag up the money and product.

"Yo Ron take this shit back to your crib and me and "D" will try to clean this shit up as best we can.'

"Aight be safe and keep your eyes open in case they double back.'

"Come on time aint with us right now. We need to hurry up." Black finished. He knew Jersey's crime rate and death toll are high. Plus the cops are as slimey as they can get. So if they'd come he would play as a witness. After D-nice finished wiping the place down with Black they crept out the back and slid around the block. They jumped in their wheels and rolled. Ron called Crock to let him know what went down.

"Hello"

"A Crock, I knew them West V. niggas were tryin to move on us. We just got in a shoot out.'

"Everybody cool?" I asked concerned.

"Naw Dame got hit and fell off the roof. Titus looked to have taken a couple clips.

"Aight look yall lay low for a while and stash the work. We gotta get yall set up in another spot up there.

"How Black and d-nice?"

"They were cleaning up the spot when I left."

"Good, good that's real good, no prints. Any witnesses?"

"Not from what I know." Ron said as he was stashing the money under a hidden door in the addict.

"Damn shitty situation huh? Let me make a couple calls right quick."

"Aight I'll holla..."

Mil and Streetz settled down on the corner of Sunset and Pine. They been ridin around in B-more for about three months and knew the streets pretty well. There was a nigga sellin on a stoop and looked to be working alone. What caught their attention was how often he would go back and fourth through this house.

"Yo, you see this shit?' Streetz asked.

"Motha fuckin right next time he go in I'ma park right there." Mil said as he pointed behind the Lincoln town car.

"We can wait on him to go re-up again and play like fiends to get the jump on him." Soon as Mil finished his statement that nigga ran back in the crib.

"Come on!" they both jumped out of the car and walked up to his spot and began to act like sensible drunks. He came back out and asked what they needed. He pulled out a couple of valves a few bags and a thing of hash.

"Pick your pleasure." He said

"We want it all nigga!" Mil & Streetz said simultaneously as they pulled their hammers out. Feelin he was caught slippin he gave everything up. No need to be killed over some replaceable shit. They took him in the crib and seen he was busy. The dining room table was loaded with money but the product was low. Mil asked

"Who you working for?" As he put his Glock 17 to his temple.

"Tori man! You aint gotta do this cause I gave you everything." He pleaded.

"Tori? Where she from?" Streetz asked.

"She holdin West V. down man."

"Stop bitchin we may let you live. Do she be in these parts?"

Mil continued his interrogation.

"Naw she send some nigga named Ricky through to collect. He was here about an hour ago. He'll be back in another hour and a half." Streetz chimed in with, "Looks like we'll be here for a while" hitting the man over the head with the gun rendering him unconscious. Mil wasted no time finding rope and tape to tie him up, they threw him in the closet and covered him with cloths and shit. They bagged the money and put it in the car as Mil shut the trunk and said, "We can rock this lil nigga who gonna miss him? Why risk running into him again?" "I feel you. We can wait to at least see his face when he comes."

"Aight"

They got in the car and listened to the radio as they watched the fiends flood the spot snatching all the drugs they could...

"They still there?"

"Yeah the last one just came back from the store."

"Aight, We about five minutes out, Yo, you and cash hit the back as soon as we pull up. Tell Cash to rush the kitchen soon as we set."

"Aight."

Hanging up the phone Rell Said. "They still in the crib so let's make haste." Rell had Ant and Buck with him and smooth was ridin with James. Pulling up to the complex they all jumped out of there cars. Tone and Cash did as they were told and ran straight to the back without hesitating. James fell in with them as they turned around the corner of the house. Rell, Buck, Smooth, and Ant were all at the front. Ant and Smooth were to cover Rell and Buck. They counted to three and rushed the door with there guns drawn. They shot at the first people they saw. The element of surprise always works to a mans favor. They were to cover Rell and Buck. They counted to three and rushed the door with there guns drawn. They shot at the first people they saw. The element of surprise always works to a mans favor. They caught three niggas sittin at a table playing dominos. Two got shot in there solar plexus as the third tried to dip out the way and had his face pealed off. Buck slid behind a wall on the west side of the building as Rell took the east side. Rell peeked around the wall and a shot rang out. Rell got hit and fell to the ground. Cash ran in as soon as he heard shots, but was sure to stay low. The kitchen had two niggas hiding from the shots, Rell and Buck let out. The shots muffled the crash of the door a little bit, but they were late on their draws.

"Die pussies." Cash yelled as he unloaded both his guns into the West Virginians. When he was sure they were dead he got low and called out to Tone and James.

"Yo these niggas gone in here, I hear movement upstairs so watch your tops." Buck continued through the house cautiously. He made his way to the kitchen and called for Cash.

"Yo come on we gotta check upstairs."

"Aight." Cash said as he finished reloading his two nines. They both moved slowly towards the steps and peeked quickly to be sure it was cleared. Buck seen it was and headed up with both guns at the ready. James came in and followed suit as did Smooth. Ant addressed Rells wounds finding only a gash where the bullet traveled across the side of his face, from the corner of his left eye to the top of his ear. It wasn't bleeding bad but it looked painful as hell. Rell was trying to cover his face as Ant was helping him to the car. At the top of the steps Buck and Cash took opposite directions. Cash seen two niggas tryin to strap themselves so he rushed them bustin his guns. He dropped one with three shots to the back, but only spun the other which allowed him to let off two shots of his own hitting Cash in his stomach and shoulder. Cash fell into the fetal position and started yelling. James came over the top of him and finished the second dude off. Buck found his section of the house clean.

"Come on Ya'll, we out! A James grab Cash and bring him to the car." Buck ran down the steps and yelled for Tone to come on. Buck jumped into the car with Ant and Rell and drove to the hospital to drop Rell off. Smooth was waiting for James and Cash to get in, then followed Ants car leaving Tone to bring up the rear of the crew...

Chapter 8

"Aight girls." Meme said. "I gotta go cause I gotta take a shower."

"Aight girl you take care of your self and try to call your man again." Mel said. Meme got up and put her coat on and made sure to show love to all her girlfriends before leaving.

"What time the baby sitter off?" Tameka asked.

"At around eleven, why?" Meme replied.

"You aint tell him yet did you?"

"No! I haven't spoken to him yet to tell him. I think he come home tonight or tomorrow."

"Just go home and get your shower, make sure you call us when you get there." Mel said as she put the grease and combs back. Meme pulled the keys out and left, jumping in her new 99 lx 330 she bought about six months ago. Once she arrived at the house the baby sitter came out the house and let the baby see her mommy.

"How was she?" Meme asked.

"Fine she loved the park; oh I feed her a while ago so she may be hungry."

"Okay was she bad at all today?" Meme she asked as she reached for her baby.

"You know the usual, here, there, its just a phase. The big thing was when she shit on the carpet."

"She did what?!"

"Yeah she shit on the carpet, I cleaned it

up, but she just runs around like she owns the place." "They say Brindles do that. I should have gotten a smaller one huh?"

"If your man loves Pit bulls a red nosed Brindle Is the way to go."

"I guess you're right I just hope it won't be too much trouble."

The dog jumped into the awaiting arms of her mommy. Tail wagging with excitement. Meme made sure essence couldn't lick her face and rubbed her head. Meme got out the car and paid the sitter two fifty, for her labor and services then went into the crib. Essence followed her close all the way to the back yard. Meme put her out and got her some water and food. She closed the door and went to get her long awaited shower...

Sitting in the car for about an hour Mil became very agitated.

"Yo where this nigga at man?"

"I don't know look let's go in there right quick."

"Why?" Mil asked

"We can drop this nigga and put a D.C. tag on him."

"That shit won't work but we can still

rock him."

As they both leave the car a big Excursion pulls up. A dark skinned stepped out and walked up to the building. Mil looked at Streetz and he ran up on him from behind with his guns out. Streetz ran up on the truck to see if any one was in there. Seeing it was empty he jumped in and started rummaging through it. Finding a couple grand in the glove box and a Beretta under the driver's seat. Mil followed Ricky into the dining room and pushed him onto a couch. "What the fuck, who you?" he said as he seen the guns at the ready. "I'm your death dealer pussy. Feel lucky?" Mil said with a small grin. "Yeah well I don't know what you want so handle yours." Mil looked at him seriously and said, "You think I won't kill you? I'd kill you just to make an odd number on my body count." The tears were being held back but he broke down and told what he knew. "Yo man you aint gotta do this, I got a family. My money is in the glove box and I got a Berretta under the Driver's seat. I don't want any trouble."

"Aight I'll tell you this if it's all there I'll let you live, but if it aint I'ma kill you and your snitchin ass homie."

"Snitch! Who you talkin about?"

Mil backed up and opened the closet with his gun still drawn on his target. The dealers head was sticking out over the clothes and when he saw Ricky he passed out again.

"You know I'ma go to Tori with this right?" Mil smiled and said,

"I hope you do P.D.K. don't run from no one."

"So yall them niggas making all that noise out here? Don't worry yall be dead in a week or two" Mil tried to mask his rage and heard Streetz coming.

"Yo Mil it's all good we can roll."

"Aight he said and looked back at Ricky, we may not last the week but you gotta survive the day." Mil finished with four shots to Ricky's belly and one in each leg. As they turned for the door Streetz put three in the dealers head and left to the car. Mil jumped in the Excursion and rolled out. Streetz followed him to Philly, they went to a spot to sell the truck and split the find...

After having a long relaxing bath I decided to watch a little T.V. the news wasn't saying much, just how some nigga was found burned to death in a trunk of a car last night in Fairmount park. Following that there was a police chase some where by Conestoga projects. It was the same shit. In Mia you could find a police chase on damn near every news channel warning you to be careful if you're in the surrounding neighborhood. The phone rang bringing me out of my daze.

"Hello."

"Oh my god I finally caught you," The familiar voice spoke.

"I do apologize for my absence but who am I speaking with?" I said fucking around knowing it was Meme.

"The fucks wrong with you? Why you acting like that? I know you aint got know body over there!" She snapped.

"Calm down! I'm fucking with you stop trippin Meme."

"Meme! There you go you so fuckin stupid, this aint no fuckin Meme!" The voice said Oh shit I thought to myself.

Now I feel like a fool.
"How many chicks you be fuckin with?"
She finished.
"Only two Serena." I said taking a second
guess at it.
"Aight you know me, but who is this
Meme?"
"Don't play dumb, I told you of her in the
county."
"Yeah, yeah. So what's up? Can you come
through?"
"I aint doin shit right now. <BEEP> Hold
on that's my other line."
"Aight." Clicking over to the other line.
"Hello"
"Hey baby what you doing?" Meme asked
hoping he'd say nothing.
"Nothing right now, why?"
"Why?" she said in a tone that couldn't be
good for me.
"Your woman needs some dick plus I got
a surprise for you."
"Oh when you want me to come over?"
"Right the fuck now!!"
"Aight hold up I got another call."
Clicking over
"Yo I gotta call you later."
"Why?"

"My man was shot today!" Making
something up.
"Aight call me later."
"Aight bye."
"Hello"
"Yeah"
"Bay I'll be there in a few."
"Aight, I love you."
"I bet you do," I said and hung up. Now I
have a problem with the "L" word and the
"C" word." Love and Commitment. I
grabbed the keys and left after cutting off
the T.V....

The day was half gone and Ron has
been laid up in the crib for the majority of
it, waiting for Black and D-nice to come
through. Miranda came walking out of
the kitchen and sat on her mans lap.
"What's wrong honey?" she asked as she
lay on his chest.
"We was in a shoot out with some Wes V.
niggas this morning." He said with a low
tone of voice. Miranda looked frightened
and searched franticly over Ron's body
for injuries.
"I'm cool, I wasn't hit. Dame got rocked
on the roof, Titus too."
"Oh my God. I can't believe this!" she said

as she hugged him.

Knock, Knock, Knock the door banged loud enough to scare her. She got up and went back to the kitchen letting Ron know it was apparently for him.

"Hello!" He said as he was walking up to the door.

"Yo, it's us dawg! Open up." Black said with his deep distinctive voice.

"Aight" opening the door Ron went back to his seat on the couch. Black and D-nice walked in with their grls. Trish been with D-nice for like a year, Tikea was fuckin with Black for a year too. Once they were in they all sat together.

"You took care of the stuff?" D-nice asked.

"Yeah I stashed it but ima get rid of it tomorrow cause Crock gonna set us up somewhere else."

"Aight then, we are gonna air them West V. niggas out aint we?" D-nice asked.

"I don't know if we gonna do that now or later; we gonna wait for Crocks orders on that."

"Orders?" Black said Orders, who that nigga suppose to be to givin orders?" he asked with somewhat of an attitude.

"Yo watch your mouth motherfucka! Not only has crock looked out for us he run the team. Don't forget that shit either!" Ron snapped knowing that Black, D-nice and Fat-cCat were his responsibility. He don't want any beef with the team that put them down with the take over.

"Look I aint saying it like that. I just keep hearing his name, I aint know he started this shit." Black said trying to eat his words.

"Look dog we family here and if Crock put us in his grips through his take over he family too. So we wait to see what he want us to do first. Til then we goin to the movies. Shit I wanna see that Kong flick." D-nice said making a valiant point.

"Yeah I wanted to see that too." Tikea said as she sat on her man lap. Trish was known to be shy but d-nice loved her for her personality. He knew that shy bit only went so far. Since they met she always been a freak under the sheets.

"You wanna see that too baby girl?" d-nice asked his girl.

"I don't care as long as I'm with you I'm good." D smiled a little knowing that he was generally loved. Once everyone agreed to go they got ready to roll. Ron was waiting for Miranda to finish her touch ups and left to the cinima…

Chapter 9

At the hospital Cash layed in the ER after a half hour fighting for his life. The shot to his shoulder was treated with no problem; the trouble came from the stomach wound. The doctorsd continued to work diligently on Cash. Rell came from his examinationwith a bandage around his head covering his eye and ear. He looked like a half dressed mummy. Buck continued to grind him up calling him Cyclops and shit. Tone was just watching his man on the operating table. Smooth went home when he got a call from Meeka.Ant was trying to pull this nurse to the side and politic for her number. Buck and Tone heard some comotion and seen Cash go into cardiac arrest. The doctors were struggling to stabelize him. When he stopped seizing the continued working on him. They shot him with some kind of medication through his intraveinus. They finally removed the bullet and sewed him up the doctor came out and said,

"We stabelized him and removed the bullet. We are moving him to intensive care for recovery. You can stay but visiting hours are over at 8 pm."

"Aight Doc we'll be back tomorrow."

"Okay"

They all left and went their own ways.Rell went home thinking of how he was gonna explain his injury to his girl. Buck and James went back to the spot and finished their little bit of work they had. Ant stayed tryin his luck with the nurse as everyone else left...

After falling back for a couple Tommy was strapped and ready to roll. It took him only ten minutes to get all his work and shit together. On his way out he bumped into his man Sincere.

"What's up nigga?" Tommy asked.

"Same shit different toilet, a nigga spot trouble knowin he tryin to avoid it."

"I see you still tyin to rhyme."

"Nah not enough money for me."

"I know these Philly niggas who runnin shit all through out Philly and D.C. I can holla at them for you." Tommy said.

"I don't know I heard they ride hard on niggas out there."

"Yeah, that keeps the team tight." Sincere thought for a sec and said, "I'll let you know "T" aight?"

"Yeah, look I gotta go check some nigga off of 8th and Willow, so holla at me later."

"Aight Dog Sincere said as he gave his man some dap.

Tommy jumped in his car which was a hooked up 97 Acura Vigor and drove off to 8th street, seeing that gator was right there he slowly approached.

"A Gator?" "You got something for me?" Tommy said.

"Yeah" he looked around and dropped a brown paper bag on Tommy's lap. Looking inside brieflyTommy was satisfied. He handed him a bag of his own and told him some time next week. Gator was always good money that's why Tommy was happy he was on his team. Driving off Tommyfelt hungry as usual and went to Wendy's for a burger and frosty. He ate inside the resturant and planned his next moves...

Mil pulled up to his mans chop shop and

honked the horn. A minute later out came a short elderly lookin man with a pair of dungarees on. He had one suspender fastened and the other over his shoulder. He recognized Mil and opened the large doors. To the garage. Once he was in Mil seen Barry working under a late modeled BMW. The older man went and told Barry he had company. He rolled out from under the car and wiped his hands.

"Okay Milie Raw I see you stepped your game up to the big wheels.

"Yeah a little some-some you know how I do."

"This is a beautiful machine here, what 03' model 22 inch rims" he looked inside and smiled then continued the description.

"A couple of T.V.'s how many miles on her?" he asked

"Eighty thousand and a full tank." Mil said answering him.

"That's pretty good, so you sellin or swoppin?"

"I'm sellin it. What couldI get for it?"

"I'll give you eight grand." Barry said with a salesman pitch.

"Give me ten and we good." Mil responded "Damn Mil you drive a hard bargin. I'll give you eight and a half."

"Nine and a half."

"Look nine G's is as high as I'll go."

Mil didn't want to lose him so he agreed to the nine grand and got out the truck and jumped in the car with Streetz. They decided to go to South Street to chill for a few hours...

Rell made his way to the crib and opened the door. The aroma of cucumber melon lingered in the house. Rell wanted to serve his woman cause he's been busy the past few days. He planned on making her moan with extacy. He could hear some tunes playing in the living room.

"I'll light a thousand candles all around show me your subway and I'll come down." As he whispered the tunes of the lyrics he took his jacket off and called his girl.

"A Mel I'm home baby girl come holla at your man!" but there wasn't a response while he was preping to remove his hustlers he heard some scruffles and a few moans in the bedroom. Confused he drew his nine Millie and opened the door slowly to find two bodies fucking in his bed. Shocked and disgusted he shot a round into the air.

"The fuck you doing?" He snapped the sheets came down and their faces were revealed. Dumas was on top of what looked to be a younger version of Melonie.

"Damn dog you don't knock?" Dumas said

"Pussy you in my house! The fuck is wrong with you; I'll kill you and think nothin of it." Seeing Kenya's face Rell snapped at her.

"And where the fuck is your sister."

"I don't know she left about an hour ago. Rell I'm sorry."

"Fuck all that get yall asses out my bed and take the sheets with you." He said

"Damn you aint tell me your sister was fuckin with him." Dumas said on the way out the door. Rell couldn't believe what he just witnessed and decided to wash the matress then jump in the shower...

Finishing off the delicious meal Meme fixed I sat undressingher with my eyes. I could tell she knew what I was doing cause she began playing with her food.

"What?" she asked with a smile revealing

her dimples.

"I'm just admiring the perfection Gods bestowed me with."

"You crazy" she said as she began to blush. I got up from the table and walked over to her, she stood to meet me halfway.

"You know I got a surprise for you right?" she whispered into my ear.

"Do you?" I replied trying to hide my anxioty.

We walked over to the back door of the crib and she opened it.

"You playin games, I thought you were the surprise." I said as I held her tight in my arms.

"That's the end of the surprise." She stepped down and called out. "Essence, Essence."

There was a little ruffling on the side of the building and out popped a lovely pitbull with her little legs and red nose. "Damn aint she cute? You aint have to get her for me."

"I figure since we're not really ready for children we may as well have a dog.

I gave her a kiss and took her to the bedroom, as she was walking she unzipped her dress and let it fall to the floor. Revealing her firm round ass and I followed suit by removing my shirt and pants. When I got into the room she immediately took control of things and threw me on the bed. She slid my boxers off revealing my goods; she wasted no time and straddled me. With the skill of a pro she rode and bucked around on my dick like she was in the rodeo. I tried to roll over to get control but couldn't get her vice like grip off of me. When ever I moved she would grab my hands and buck harder, I was at the point of no return and she started to scream. "Don't stop. No please don't stop." I felt myself ready to cum and she siezed up and came right with me. That was the first time she's ever taken control in the bedroom. I was in shock cause it was different, but exhilirating.

"You know I love uyou?" she said softly. "I know that's why I can't lose you." She layed on my chest and fell asleep. I was still in shock about her performance and dozed off eventually...

Buck started his day by heading to the spot on 33rd street to see if there was

any weight to be moved. 33rd street is we also keep an inventoryof the other strips. No one but three people knew of this spot. Crock, Rell, and Buck, that way we wont have to worry about any unwanted company. After seeing that we were losing klientel in D.C. he decided to have Devin and Oscar relocate. Buck locked up and drove around town and seen who looked to be Onnie with some other nigga. As Buck got close he recognized the dark skinned man as Tank. A drug pusher from D.C. figuring Onnie was working for him, Buck pulled out his hammer and sat it in his lap and rolled up on them.
"Ayo Onnie" Buck yelled. He turned around and looked startled.
"Huh"
"Yeah nigga I knew I'd catch you slippin!" Buck pulled his gun up and trained it on Onnies head.
"You know you couldn't hide forever."
        Realizing he was caught he didn't run cause he knew Buck was a good shot. He tried to think of something to say.
"Look youngin I don't know who you are but you on my turf. This shit aint goin

down like this" Tank said as he signaled to an asian chick. She came out of the SUV with a pump. Buck wasn't worried knowing his car was armor plated. Rolling his window up a little Buck figured Onnie was Tanks right hand so he could cut the chickens head off and deal with the body later. Buck fixed his gun on Tank and shot twice. Soon as he fired he ducked down as the Asian chick shot the pump at the door as he peeled out...

Chapter 10

Smooth was on his way to collect from Reese and Twan on Frankford ave. seeing them make a couple more sales he called them over. Twan told Sid to keep collecting.

"A what up Smooth?" Reese asked giving dap.

"Aint shit I'm just collecting."

"Oh aight" Reese stood and pulled three brown bags out of his coat pocket, and gave them to Smooth. In return Smooth gave him three bags of his own.

"Good look" Smooth said "Oh keep yall

eyes peeled for those West V. niggasand them D.C. niggas too."
"Aight one."

Smooth rolled to 17th street and seen Two-Tone and Ant on the stoop.
"Ant take this in the crib for me." Smooth asked and gave him the bags.
"Aight a any word on Cash yet?"
"Nah we still waiting for them to call. Tone still there though."
"Aight I'll holla at you."
"Aight."
Smooth rode around and then planned to go to a bar to relax a bit. Then figured he'd go with Buck but he didn't answer his phone half way to Stans he called Rell up.
"Yo"
"Rell what's up?"
"Aint shit what you doing" Rell asked.
"About to go to a bar, you wanna chill today?
"Fuckin right man I just caught this nigga Dumas fuckin Melonie Sister in here."
"Stop playin"
"Seriously that shit got me fucked up right now."

"I'ma be at Stan's aight" Smooth said.
"Aight man give me a minute."

Smooth parked and went in and hollared at Stan.
"Yo Stan I'll be in the back if anyone needs me."
"Aight"
Smooth went to the booth and chilled as the waitress brought him his drink.

After sitting in the bar for about an hour Devin grew restless. He's been following this tip for the last six months on some nigga being with them Dip Set boys and followed him here. He was out side a crib that was semi-guarded and had two niggas standing post. Oscar was sleep for the past twenty minutes so he kept taking pictures of his marks last rest stop. Devin and Ocar have been working for Crock for the last year. Crock put them on them niggas who claimed the Dip Set to find their community.the thing was they seemed to reside in D.C. so Devin called his brother Oscar up and they got on their jobs. Devin examined the crib and saw it was a four story building with a ten or eleven foot gate at the front, the place didn't seem to be that well gaurded other than the front.

    "A "O"" Devin said as he tapped his brother.

"What up?"

"Take over for me; I'm trying to get some rest. That nigga went into the crib ten minutes ago and he don't look to be coming out no time soon."

"Aight" Oscar said as he got out and hopped into the front seat after Devin jumped into the passenger seat...

    Coming out of the movie theater Black and Ron were cracking up at the movie. The girls were discussing how big that nigga was and how come he fell for a white girl. As they were moving along they ran into some chic that had a little squabble with Trish a few weeks back. Trish seen the girl and without hesitation she tossed the remaining portions of her popcorn into the girls face and started whopping her ass.

"Yo what the fuck bitch you thought I forgot?!" she yelled as she landed a blow to the side of the girls head. The girl was caught off guard and fell with her three inch shoes on. Ron, Black and D-Nice couldn't believe this was the same shy

girl from prep school. Miranda was about
to jump in but Ron pulled her back
seeing Trish had the fight won. Some
nigga came running up on the girls and
Black jumped in his way revealing his
holstered P-90 and said,
"Listen my man you aint got shit to do
with this!"
"Look nigga that's my wife and she's
pregnant!"
D-nice over heard and quickly jumed on
his job and pulled his girl off the woman.
Black helped the girl to her feet and
asked,
"Are you okay" as sincerely as he could.
"I'll be fine thanks" she said with a few
scrapes on her face. Black turned around
and couldn't see D-Nice and Trish but did
see Ron keeping motha fuckas back.
When she seemed calm they too left.
Black knew it wasn't his place but he
asked any way.
"What was that all about if you don't
mind my asking?"
"No I don't mind, that is about sibling
rivary and yes she, Trish or what the
family calls her Trisha is my sister. My
mom died about a month ago and left the

house to me."

"So this is about the house I presume?" Black asked.

"No this is about me" the man said.

"And who are you?"

"Jarvise or J.D. I use to go out with Trisha and had made a bad decision and cheated on her. After she left me I met Tiffany and we got engaged."

"And that's why she's upset. We were and we made a pat that we wouldn't mess with each other's exes until three months passed. I couldn't wait and now I am pregnant so we got engaged."

"Damn Black said as he heard the story of another disfunctional family.

Tiken came over and put her hands around her man and asked, "Are we leaving soon I am cold?"

"I'm sorry baby I'm ready turning to Jarvis, "look I'm sorry about all thisbut if you take my number I'm sure we can get them to squash this."

"Aight" Black gave him his number and left thinking he could use that blue colar nigga in the long run. On the way back Trish was crying her eyes out. D-Nice didn't understand let alone know what to do. He tried to console her with "baby I'm sorry's, I love yous, and it'ds gonna be okays."

When they reached the house she looked exhausted and she looked depressed D-Nice was once known for finding ways to cheer a woman up. he got out of the car and opened her door; she looked up with a distant stare. He picked her up and kicked the car door closed and carried her to the door. He fumbled with the keys until he got the door open, then carried her in and kicked the door close. Once inside he went straight to the bed room and layed her on the bed. That's when it seemed the life started to come back.

"No I'm not tired." But D-Nice payed her no attention and began taking her shoes off followed by her jacket.

"Darrius stop it. I told you I'm not tired." She said with a scuff as if she's been drinking. Yet again D-Nice continued to dis robe her. When she was in her panties he slid them down and she began to squirm but to no avail. He layed between her legs and began to suck on her clit while holding her legs open with his arms. When she started to moan that's when he got in a better position and held her pussy lips open with his left hand and licked her clit as he fingered the moistening love box. After about five minutes she was ranting and yelling. "Oh my God right there! Don't stop! Please don't stop! Aah! She screamed as she reached multiple orgasms and clamped tighrt around D-Nices' head. "Promise you'll never leave me!" she said before being subdued by the sandman. D-Nice put the quilt over her and jumped in the shower...

"Rell Yo what's the deal?" Stan asked as he walked in the lounge.

"Same shit, different toilet."

"A some chic named Kenya was lookinfg for you."

"Aight that's my lil sista she probably want money."

"Don't know!"

Rell continued to his favorite booth and ordered a couple of cheese burgers and cokes. As the waitress left Rell chilled and watched the bar begin to fill up. he caught a couple chics observing him in the booth one even came up and asked to chill. He had to let her know it was boy's dayout and he was waiting for someone. But she sat anyway.

"So how does a woman like me find a nighga like you?" she said as she leaned ove the table trying to show excessive clevage.

"Look ma I don't know what you would need to do. But you need to try on another nigga cause this one's taken." Not seeing Smooth standing there Rell looked a bit startled when he heard, "Oh shit! That was some shit straight out of a comic book or something." Sitting down Smooth looked at the semi-attractive woman and introduced himself.

"I'm Smooth and this stuck up ass nigga is Rell" Rell had the lookion his face like he ate something he shouldn't have and jumped in,

"She was just leaving weren't you?" ignoring him she gave her name.

"I'm Christina and I was tryin to holla at your man but he claims he spoken for. Shit one thing I know about the market is everything has it's price."Smooth looked at Rell and said with a grin,

"So what's your price?" then broke out

laughing. Just what Smooth needed to clear his mind of the episode he seen today. I don't want to intrude so I'll leave my number here on the table so if I get a call we'll go from there." As she got up she dropped her number on the table and neither of them moved. The waitress came in with Rell's food and set it in front of him.

"Damn nigga you knew I was coming you could have at least ordered me something. Selfish ass nigga." No sooner than him finishing his sentence another burger and coke came in. Rell just looked at him. Don't choke on the laces trying to leave room for the burger." Laughing hysterically at the dumb ass look on Smooths' face. They started to eat and begaun toplan out the days activities. In between bites Smooth asked,

"Have them niggas Reese and Sid been holding shit down?"

"yeah they tight plus they don't tolerate any B.S."

"That's whjat's up they better not."

Rell made a mental note to find out what Devin and oscar found out about that nigga "E"...

Chapter 11

After riding around for a minute checking a few niggas my cell rang.

"Yo"

"A when you coming back down to see me?" I recognized the voice but couldn't pinpoint who.

"Down where?! You know a nigga do a lot of traveling." Trying not to sound out there.

"Your crib on the beach, you do know who this is don't you?" then it hit me.

"Come on Lala you know a nigga couldn't forget somethingas precious as you."

"So when you coming back." She asked turning her accent on full blast."

"I don't know yet but I'll let you know ma."

"Aight call me."

"I will." Then I hung up. I was on my way to holla at Miranda then remembered that I had to holla at Stretch. He may know something about them West V. niggas and them piss pet niggas.the ride was about ten minutes then I got the P3. The place was laxed and mellow. I got in and was greeted by Stretch and a few dancers.

"What's the deal Crock!"

"Aint shit but we need to talk."

Seeing that I asked to talk he knew that I needed info in other words. We went up to his private room and I asked.

"You now about them niggas that been reppin West V.?"

"I know who run it and some rumors."

"Rumors?"

"Yeah Tori she was suppose to be this bitch that fucked with this nigga from New York some big time nigga Tru-Blu"

"Q"

"Yeah you know him?"

"I know of him" trying not to say much.

"Well she stole a hundred keys and about two hundred grand then left to Wes V. and opened up major."

"He aint go after her?"

"I don't know but she's a slouch word is she lives in a condo in VA. By the Chesapeak river."

"And no one tried to drop her and her tam?"

"Niggas scared of that New York nigga."

"So what up with them Dip niggas?"

"They done. People screamin they name but it's just to make shit sound good they had little niggas trying to bring back the team but failed."

"Aight my niogga I need to check another spot here." I handed him a grand and left to holla at Miranda. Being as though it was a five minute drive I didn't even bother with the radio. Walking into the bar the place looked real slow for a Wednesday. I went straight to the bar and sat.

"A what's up Crock?" Mike asked as he was preping a drink for some one.

"Could I get you anything?"

"Nah I just wanted to holla at Miranda for a minute."

"Oh she's probably in the back she'll be out in a second."

"Aight" as I waited I wondered if any of these niggas could be affiliated with them niggas from Wes V. or Piss Pets.

Continuing to look around I didn't even notice Miranda was standing behind me. Clearing her throat she said,

"What's going on Crock?"

Oh shit my bad you got a minute?"

"Yeah I can talk follow me."

She showed me to a booth in the far right hand corner of the bar and we sat. seeing that she looked a bit tired I didn't want to be long.

"I see you still wear tight fitted cloths."

"Sometimes you gotta get the tips flowin."

"I feel you , a do you still see them Dip niggas?" I asked as I kept l;ooking throught the mirrors on the wall to watch myself.

"Nah the last time I heard of them was about six months ago but that was it."

"Aight , look if you hear anything about them or some Wes V. shit let a nigga know!"

"Aight I gotta get back to work."

"Aight then, stay beautiful."

She laughed as she got up. I followed her lead and left the bar. I figured Buck or Rell might have heard something so I headed to the hut on 33rd...

There was a brisk chill coming from the spine of Mil like something wasn't right. But he continued to walk to the strip with his man. Streetz found himself occupied with an attractive woman in front of a steak house. Mil didn't wanna

cock block so he walked up a little and
stood by a corner. As he stood there he
got that feeling again but this tyime he
grabbed his piece. His eyes grew wiery
and started to looke back and forth
through the crowd and then he seen it.
The barrel of a gun and a man standing
behind it with the look of death. Instint
kicked in and Mil and tried to duck out of
the way and heard a loud Boom! Boom!
With the panic of the crowd Mil couldn't
see were Streetz was so he tried to find
the gunman before he was found.
Jumping to his feet he dipped back and
forth throught the crowd and seen Streetz
standing stiff as a board with that same
bitch.
"Something aint right about this shit" he
said to himself as he ran up behind them
drawing his gun. When he got closer he
could see she had a gun to his back. With
one motion he grabbed her gun which
spu her and shot two rounds into her
exposed chest. Streetz was still
bewildered about being caught off guard.
Mil's adreniline was still racing as they
made their way to their car. No sooner
then Streetz put the key in the door two

SUV's pulled up next to them. Feeling they may not live through this they simultaniously started shooting at the SUV's when they opened the sliding doors. They shot about four people but the number of these niggas was overwhelming. Streetz was shot three times and fell between two cars. Mil was trying to run around a car for some cover but was hit in the head due to ricoche. One of the shooters jum0ped out of the car and dropped a note on Streetz's body then they left...

The day has been long and strenious Tommy decided to go home and chill after he made a couple more pickups. On his way to Christian st. he noticed some new niggas pushing right were his youngin Miz supposed to be. Being as though most niggas knew him he rolled up on them.

"A who the fuck yall suppose to be?" he asked with his usual aggressive nature. "Listen old timer this a new day cop and roll or get served our way." Feeling like he had to teach this little nigga Tommy pulled his 45 and shot the kid twice in the chest and rolled out. Looking through his mirrors to see if he was followed, he caught West Virginia plates on a blue Pontiac GTO. Still worrying about the cops tommy rolled to the crib once he was sure he wasn't followed and took a shower. After the shower he still was concerned about who that lil nigga was so he put a bug out. Tommy finished getting dressed and grabbed the phone.

"Hello"

"A it's me."

"What's up T? you chillin?" the voice said.

"Naw I just popped some nigga up on 16th and Christian and he had some West Virginia plates on his car."

"West Virginia I don't know of any...Oh hold up word was some niggas were down South Street with some Wes V. plates in a shooting."

"When you hear this?"

"On the news like ten minutes ago. But that was on South Street in Philly. I aint hear shit about them in Norristown."

"Aight look keep your head down and ears open for me."

"Aight." Tommy layed on the couch and watched the news to see what was what...

Chapter 12

Buck was still a little anxious about the shooting a bit earlier but knew if that nigga was running shit it's now up to Onnie to explain what went down. Buck wanted to chill but felt like driving around anyway so he called Rell.
"Yo"
"What up Rell, what you up to?" Buck asked.
"Me and Smooth chillin down here at Stans, why what's up?"
"You'll never guess who I just ran into."
"Who nigga? You know I don't fuck with guessing games." Rell said with a bit of flair
"Onnie! He was with some nigga down on 8th and Diamond."
"Yeah, I know you got at him!"
"Nah that nigga was claiming he ran that strip and played tough when I had my hammer in that nigga face.
"Damn who was he?" Rell asked
"I don't know but he aint gonna be runnin shit any more."
"So what you doin now?"
"I'm about to go to the detail shop to

check on these rim I got made for Jas."
"Yeah it's like that huh? Just keep your head nigga. You know we got niggas after us it seems."
"Yeah, we need to got o them niggas and run fire on their block. Matter of fact why don't we have a meetin at the spot tonight with Crock and the others." Buck suggested.
"Why you know something?"
"I will tonight when Devin and Oscar check in."
"I'll call Crock and the others later on."
"Aight Dog I'll holla at you laterBuck said as he hung up.
　　　Buck turned onto Ogantz and pulled into the parking lotof the detail shop. Getting out of the car Buck could see a set of the rims he had ordered in the window and felt excited to see them finished. Walking in he was greeted.
"Yo papi what's up?"
"Aint shit Los I see you finished the rims."
"You know we play no games papi, when you need them?"
"I'll bring the car around later about two o'clock."

"Okay papi I'll be here oh I gotta show you something."
"What up?"

They walked to the back of the detail shopand Carlos revealed a Jaguar X-Type with the doors strippedand showing some keys of cocain glued to the inner walls of the doors.

"Damn Los" Buck said and continued with,

"Where you get this shit that's like forty grand right there."

"This new Jack came to me with this car and asked me to paint the car a metallic coat and we stripped it and found this."

"Where they from?"

"They plates say West Virginia but he looked funny like he was nervous."

"Did he show you any I.D. or an address?"

"Yeah I got a copy in the other room."

"Bet let me peep that."

"Aight"

As they walked back into the other room Carlos continued saying that Buck was the only one he could tell with out having the police involved.

"Here it is papi."

Buck looked and copied down the address and thought to himself with this information he had what he needed to drop the bombshell on them pussies...

Ron has been sitting around the house for the majority of the afternoon. He flipped throught the channels and seen "South Street Massacre" and turned it up.

"This just in, on the night of Wednesday July forth there was a massacre on South Street. Twelve were pronounced dead. There is however a search for two late modeled black Sprt Utility Vehicles. Witnesses say the vehicles had West Virginia license plates. If you have any information on the wereabouts of these vehicles please call the hot line shown at the bottom of the screen. Please by any means don't come within a reasonable distance of them. They are presumed armed and dangerous."

"Damn" Ron said to himself as he heard the news. Knowing these niggas is getting real cocky with it. He turned the television down and kept thinking that they had to be dealt with fast before they caught up to them. He reached for the phone and called D-Nice.

"Yo what it be" D-Nice answered

"Same shit" did you see the news?"

"Naw why?"

"Them Wes V. niggas just killed like twelve people down on South Street."

"Stop playin" D-Nice said as he brushed the accusation off.

"Nigga this shit real they dumped on us and we barley made it out"

"True that! But you really think it's them niggas?" Ron became aggitated and said, "Look nigga we tight but you getting me mad. These pussies aint playin, they on some murder one shit. I'ma go to Wes V. and start droppin them fools the same way they droppin us."

"Damn nigga you serious?" D-Nice realizing that he may have to ride out.

"You motherfuckin right nigga is you ridin or what?"

"Nigga don't disrespect! You know I'm with you. You gonna call Black or you want me to?"

"Go ahead and let him know I'ma get more niggas to ride with us."

"Aight nigga get at me."

"Aight"

Ron sat on the couch for about another ten minutes thinking of who he could call. Knowing Titus and Dame already got rocked he needed some loyalniggas to ride with him who aint gonna bitch up. he remembered two other young niggas that have been getting their hustle on but couldn't be making much from that sceme. If they hit a couple spots hard they could come up. Getting up from the couch he walked to the window and peered out. Looking at the corner he seen little activity, but could sense he would have to bring at least three or four niggas with them!

After following the movements of this nighga for about six or seven months Devin figured his pattern out real quick. He liked to go to the "Y" in the mornings and work out then he'd go to the bar till about eleven or twelve. At around twelve thirty or one he would visit his family members in the old folks home in D.C. Maryland. At three he would go to what looked to be his brothers' home. And from five to late night he would be with his homies and then he'd go home. Once he was greeted by his "team" they would all pass him knots of money. He'd count it up and then he'd nod. So he might be running things. They all liked to stay at this condemed apartment on the corner of Penn and 120th there was about eight of them not counting this nigga. Devin and Oscar already made plans to figure this niggas handle out but it couldn't be hard.

"You think this be that nigga everyone talkin about?"

"Who that?"

"This nigga we following?" Oscar asked with his slured speech.

"Who E or Erin?" Devin asked

"Yeah"

"I don't know, if it is they may be the last of his team." Devin said as he eyed his mark.

"You know we can find out." Devin looked at Oscar with a bewildered expression.

"How?"

"One of us can go to the old folk's home and ask to see the log book. They have to sign in and if he did we know what time he went."

"I'm glad you my brother I'll drop you off when he leaves he going there in about

ten or fifteen muinutes any way."
"Aight" Oscar said with a bit of a smile.
Devin liked the plan and decided to go
through with it. As they followed him to
the spot Oscar jumped out and followed
at a good distance. Devin just hoped his
peoples stayed safe...

Sitting in a leather sofa seat I
continued to smoke my blint and passed
it. I've been smokin for a minute and the
effects don't seem to hit me hard any
more unless I had some knock you out
shit!
"A son, so how you wanna do this kid
from D.C.?" "Q" asked
"We got niggas on him now but it's the
Wes V. motha fuckas that's been causing
problems FAM.
"Yeah I could have my man help yall out
if you want." "Q" said
"That's cool you know how we do, this
situation is under hand. I got my men on
both of them and we may move real soon.
That pussy in D.C. is beginning to slip." I
said
"Aight that's what I'm talkin about." He
said as he took another toke and said,
"Handle yours my nigga." As he passed

the blint back.over the months me and "Q" been real close to the point a nigga may call us partners. Nah we justtight that's all. Plus I like his style and I've been planning to hit Harlem real soon. They may be movin some shit but they all some pretty niggas. I don't think they can handle pressure. I just gotta pick the right time is all.

"So you gonna handle that forty for me?" asked "Q"

"Yeah I'll do that right now, cause I can kill two birds with one stone."

I grabbed my cell and called Rell up.

"Hello"

"A Rell what it is my nigga?" I said jokingly

"Crock what the fuck is wrong with you? What you high?"

"A little, look I'm in M.Y. and I need you to bring forty for me."

"When, cause I'm on the other line with Devin and he got "E" out there slippin."

"Yeah" I covered the phone and told "Q" 'A they got this nigga slippin now."

"Who"

"That D.C. nigga" talkin back into the phone I said,

"A Rell we gonna take this nigga tonight so have the boys get ready and we doing it late night so tell them to grip them silencers."

"Aight that's what the fuck I'm talkin about."

"Have Ant and Two-Tone handle that thing and tell Devin to keep his eyes open it's tonight."

"Aight"

As I hung up the phone I felt his eyes on me so I said "how's handled sound." He just looked at me like he didn't know me. Or more like feared me.

"It's like that?" he asked throught the tokes of the blunt.

"Yeah it's like that. A I gotta run and get shit poppin so I'll hit you up when I can."

"Aight"

I got up and headed towards my car when I felt a strange feelinglike I was being watched but I was high so I said fuck it. I got in the car and drove to the crib to get some sleep before we moved on this nigga...

Chapter 13

Rell finished up his call with Buck and Smooth. He was sure to tell them that it was on tonight when Crock came through. They were to call Two-Tone, Ant and James. Smooth already called Sid, Twin and Reese. So the team would pretty much be there. Rell was already eating cause Melanie cooked some shit. She'd have a fit if he didn't eat after she cooked, he told everyone to be at the spot around ten o'clock tonight cause word is that's when that nigga gets home. Rell finished his food and looked at his watch 8:30. Aight I got time. He wanted to grab some shit off his man. He's been buying bullets from this nigga who had the works. He was an ex-Marine and he had a basement full of guns, ammo, grenades, all types of shit, plus he aint charge too much. Well to me he didn't. he was about a forty five minute drive so Rell made sure he had about ten grand on him. Pulling up to the crib Rell beeped his horn twice at the garage. The door opened and he drove in. when he cut the car off he seen him in the corner of the garage.

"Rell my main man." He yelled and I

mean yelled.

"Rambo what it be? Rell asked

"Same shit, reloadin nines and killin time."

"Ha, you my dude. A I need a lot of shit man," cutting to the point.

"Hoorah, that's why I like you Captain straight to the point. Got some major Bang-Bang coming huh?" he asked with alittle excitement.

"Yeah we gotta a major hit coming I'ma nee like eight vests, 2 HKs ,2 Aks, 2 MP5 and 2 Barrels for the K's, 5 Bananna clips for the HKs, 5 one hundred shot clips for the MP5s and some granades." Rell said as he was coming off the top.

"Holy mother of Joe, fucking with pam in the city of Toledo! You aint got a Bang-Bang you have a war on your hands. Need any extra help?" he asked excitedly.

"Nah man we need you to stay alive you are our supply man. You know our gizmo nigga."

"Aight" they went to the basement through his secret wall and grabbed the stuff and put them in the car. Rell thought he may need shells for the hand held's so he grabbed rounds for the .45s

and .40s nines, 357s and the eagles.
"That's a hell of a lot of fire [power man
you sure you don't need any help?"
"We cool what I owe you?" Rell asked.
"Give me seventy five hundred and we
even."
"Aight Rell gave him eight grand and left."
On the trip back Rell obeyed every
fucking traffic law there was like Miss
Daisy type shit. Once he got to the spot it
was about ten minutes after ten. He then
put everything out on the tablehe put the
bullits out as well and that's when he
started to load his clips...
"Ooh baby that's how I like it" cooed
Tikea as her and Black were going
through one of their sexcapades.
"Like this?" Black asked as her drove
himself deeper.
"Aah that's the spot keep it gpoing." She
moaned. Black was dickin her with her
ankles by her head and she layed wide
open for him. She couldn't take much
dick when they first met but after a
couple fuck episodes she's as limber as a
gymnist. He pounded her pussy for at
least five minutes like that then flipeped
her five foot two frame and slide his dick

in from behind. She met instant gratification and began to have an orgasm. Black felt himself spasm and started to speed up.

"Oh my God! You got the magic dick make me scream." Black began a pace that a marathon runner couldn't keep. Then he nutted while she was in her second orgasm. Soon as he finished he went to the bathroom to get a quick shower. Tikea layed in the bed exhausted. The phone rang about four times then stopped. Black yelled from the shower, "Who was it?" But he got no response. He was in the shower laughing how he put her to sleep. Then the phone rang again, Black rinsed off then jumped out of the shower to answer the phone.

"Hello?"

"Black what it be?" D-Nice asked through the music in the background.

"Aint shit, were you at?"

"I'm at this club that just opened up called the happy ending."

"Yeah where that's at?" Black askedas he continued to dry himself off.

"You can't miss it, it's like three spots from the Eutopia: Plus Ron wanted us to ride with him to Wes V.to handle that bitch Tori. Or some shit."

"We'll talk about it in a minute I just got out of the shower give me about five minutes."

"Aight"

Black started to put lotion on and got dressed. He was out the door in no time. Arriving outside the club a valet offered his services to Black. Black got out his car, Baby blue BMW 7 series, and got a stub in return. Walking in the spot which was jumpin. Black knew he wouldn't find D-Nice in there so he called his cell.

"Yo"

"A nigga were you at?" asked Black through the noise.

"Look up; I'm up stairs by the rail. What you just come in?"

"Yeah." Black looked up and saw D-Nice waving in the corner of the club so he made his way there.

"A what's up my man?" D-Nice asked as he dapped his man up.

"You know me doin me, had to lay that pipe down, now Tikea sleep in the bed."

"Okay look, right you wanna roll with

em?" cutting right to important matters
"Yeah that's our man, but how he gonna set it up?"
"He said he gonna holla at one of their cronies and set up a big buy." D-Nice explained
"Okay so he gonna get her out of her own?"
"Yeah then we gonna get strapped and he gonna lay her out and we take out the surrounding niggas."
"I like how it sound when he wanna do this?" Black asked
"I don't know probably soon."
"Aight I'm down."
"Aight bet, it's on then."

They both went back to enjoy the drinks and the music...

Tommy got off his ass and went to the window, wasn't shit happening. So he went to check on this bitch he used as personal information rep. he got in the car and drove about three blocks to where they usually meet but this time she didn't come out. He beeped the horn about three times then decided to go in. Knowing the area Tommy pulled his P89 out and knocked on the door. After knocking about twice the door cracked opened and there was Adrian.

"What you aint hear me?" he said on the other side of the door trying to look into the crib.

"I wasn't tryin to come out today." She said with a look that could only mean she was not alone.

"You aight in there or you want me to come back?"

"I'll manage." She responded and Tommy slowly turned around. He knew something was up so when she closed the door, he turned around and waited till he felt she was away from the door and kicked it open. Tommy rushed into the living room and seen two unfamiliar faces and shot both of them twice in the chest and one in the face. He was rushing around to see who else was in there and seen the bedroom door closed. He opened the door and seen a bad ass chic naked in the bed. He may have hesitated too long cause soon as he closed the door behind him he heard a shot. He looked down and seen it wasn't from his gun, and looked up to see a hole the size of a nickel in his chest smoking. He looked up to see who shot him and Adrian was standing there with a .45 caliber hand gun in her hand. Although she was shaking tears in her eyes Tommy tried to lift his gun but was met with another round to the stomach. Shocked he was caught by a chic he thought wouldn't cross him the pain started to kick in. he tried to yell from the pain of his heart exploding but all that came out was gurgles. As he was drowning in his blood he was saying to himself I was dropped by a bitch...a bitch...

Oscar was driving around as the tail as Devin took some more notes on "E". They were waiting till he did his usual routine then headed home to let the others know. This time he seemed to be inviting people to the crib. There were about two or three people following him home. Once they got there it was official that it was a party. There were about twenty people in all, dressed like it was a college party. They all looked to be on his payroll. Devin said they'd wait it out. "Fuck that those pussies all claim that dip shit so let them all get dipped in shit" Oscar yelled

"Aight Fuckit" Devin grabbed his cell phone and called Rell

"Yo"

"A Rell these niggas here and they having a party these faggots don't even look prepared for some heavy shit." Devin said rousing himself up.

"Bet I'll call you in five be by the phone."

"Aight"

Devin told Oscar in about five, then they waited and watched as they all went into the semi-mansion the only thing was the two who usually stand post were nowhere to be found and the gate stayed open. Devin thought to himself "these niggas got caught with their pants down!"...

Chapter 14

Drivin around a bit even though I don't even know how I got into the car in the first place. I must have been smoking that shit again. Feelin a lil bit better cause we about to handle that D.C. nigga I listen to that fifty cent "many men" on C.D. on my way to my crib I wanted to get a shower I see the block was filled and I had to park on the corner again. As I got out I seen this nigga Lester whose been look out for me for a while.

"A Lester", I yelled "let me holla at you for a second." Lester looked a little paranoid and acting a bit off. I only wanted to talk. He think I wanna hurt him cause he made my girl fall knowing she pregnant. As he came over he started his shit.

"A Crock, look man, my bad. I aint mean it." He pleaded.

"Look its cool nigga she aight and the baby cool, I just wanted to know if you seen Rell come through?"

"Naw" he said with a look of relief

"Aight look when you see him tell him to holla at me."

"Aight" I walked back up the block and seen a nigga runnin towards me with a big ass trench on like he about to miss his bus. When he got close I stepped to the side to let him pass but he stopped next to me.

"A homie you got the time on you?" in a familiar voice. Paying it on mind I say "Yeah I got you." I looked down at my watch and seen it was two thirty. I don't think the bus come yet." I said as I started to look up I seen the nigga pull his coat open and reveal a sawed off side by side gauge BOOM! The sound was deafening from this range and the force from the blast threw me against a car and to the ground, I couldn't feel any pain which I couldn't understand. I felt around me and shit was all slimy, I grabbed something that was solid and looked at it. It had to be either my stomach or my kidney cause it looked funny. My eyes started to blur in and out of vision, I could feel my heart slowing in rhythm. I said to myself "how could I get caught slippin so late in the game?" then this nigga stood over me, he had some kind of hoodie on and I couldn't see his face. From the way his head was moving I could tell he was saying something. I could only get pieces.

"Xxxx xxxx you gonna do xxx xxxxx? Payback xxxx xx x bitch?" BOOM!!!

"Aah! I jumped out of bed sweating like an African doing mother fuckin somersaults through the Sahara. "Damn what type of shit is that?" I asked myself. A nigga can't even sleep without having nightmares. I got in the shower for about ten or fifteen minutes. When I got out the clock blinked ten thirty, I finished getting dressed and grabbed my keys and cell then left to the meet. On the way I seen I had a couple messages on my cell so I listened to the first one.

"Yo nigga it's Rell were you at? We here waiting for you at the spot get your ass outta bed!" BEEP...this nigga bitchin and I'm on my fuckin way. The second on was Meme.

"Hey boo I've been waiting on you to come over all day. I hope you okay cause I got some good news. I know it's gonna make yourday. I wanted to wait till I seen you but I can't wait. I'm pregnant with your child! Your child!("I hope it's mine I said with excitement"I can't wait to see...BEEP...I know she hated that you can never get a whole message out on them machines. I pulled up to the spot and went in the crib. The first thing I seen was a table filled with guns, ammo and some grenades.

Rell was there at the table with Smooth, Sid, and Reese. Ant was walking out of the kitchen with a sandwich.

"What's up Crock?" he yelled as did

everyone else.

"Chillin, my bad if I'm late." I said

"It's your operation so I start when you show." James said sitting on the couchplaying Madden with Two-Tone and Twan.

"Where's Buck?" I asked

"He aint come yet." Rell said

"Aight a look, Rell did you hear anything from Dev or Los?"

"Yeah, they at that nigga spot keepin tabs they said he havin a party and all his croonies there. Plus they not strapped."

"That's good, that's real good; we get pass the two guards out side and we..."

"Nah they at the party too," Rell cut me off and said. "Damn, all we waitin on is Buck?"

Soon as I said that Buck came waltzing in the crib.

"A I got that address on them Wes. V. niggas I know we gonna handle that?"

"Look we'll give that to Ron and Black to get them on that shitwe gotta handlethis shit right here. Now!" I said and continued

"look when we get there we goin in three in the front and two gonna watch the doors. Matter of fact Dev and Los will watch the doors. Me, Twan, James, Smooth, and Sid will hit the front. Two-Tone you Rell, Buck, Reese, and Ant hit the back."

"Wouldn't that cause cross fire?" Twan asked

"Nah his mission is build where the main floor is a level higher. So yall pretty much will be coming in from the basement."

"So how you wanna do this Crock just run in and blaze the place or what?" Rell asked.

"Not at all we gonna position ourselves outside and throw like ten grenades then we go in and drop anything movin, anything!"

"Damn that's smooth." James interjected.

"Yeah I wanna leave that place hollow as hell. Everyone grip what you gonna use and let's go.

Everyone started reaching for guns Rell already had his AK47 with a barrel drum. Smooth and Buck grabbed an HKS with some clips and I grabbed four magazines for my glock .40's James grabbed the other AK with the barrels, and everyone grabbed like two green bandits. Within no time we were on the road...

Jasmin came out of the kitchen with a big bowl of popcorn and two liter soda for the movie.

"Damn girl you got it all huh?" Meeka asked

"Come on girl, you know that nigga takes care of me girl." Jas said "That nigga love me."

"Bitch all our men take care of us, I don't know what you tryin to say." Mel said with her usual North Philly flair.

"Damn what's gotten your pussy so red?" Meme asked

"I told yall I don't like that scary shit and yall get 'The Haunting' and 'Candy man'."

All of the women broke into laughter cause they knew she aint like them.

"Come on now 'Candyman' aint scary." Jas said

"Fuck if it aint." Mel said

Meme put the 'Candyman' in and played it, they all got quiet and begun to watch the movie. Mel went and grabbed a blanket from the closet and sat at the foot of the sofa and tried to deal with the flick...

Chapter 15

Ron was getting in the car after talking to his young nigga Swift and Chaz. They wanted to ride with him but they wanted to get some of the money and other shit but they missed the whole point of the set up, so he chose to cut them out. Riding Buck to his crib his phone rang.

"Yo what's the deal?"

"A Ron I got an address on them Wes. V. niggas so you can move on them when you can." Buck said

"We about to move on them already we set a meet through her pusher at like eleven thirty twelve."

"Damn that's good money."

"A we hndlin somethin so let me know."

"Aight"

Not even ten minutes passed before his phone rang again.

"Hello"

"I'm on my way to the meet now how about you?" the woman asked

"Yeah I'll be there before you know it." They hung up and Ron called his boys.

"A what's up." D-Nice asked

"What the fuck nigga you gotta meet me at my crib in a couple."

"Bet we'll be there."

"Aight

Ron went into the crib and he already had the money sorted in his briefcase with his .45 under a couple bills.he had two other cases custom built AK's inside, if you hit the button the case will drop and the guns will be revealed. But you can also open the case with a four digit code and it'll look to be a regular case. He filled them with money and waited about ten minutes till D-Nice and Black came in.

"Damn nigga she in a fuckin hurry aint she?" yelled D-Nice.

"That's those cases we had with the H Kisles in them?" Black asked

"Yeah"

"A we gonna go in there and handle this shit when I say my supplier told me to tell you something." That's when yall drop any of them niggas they got as body guards. She told me she got four people with her but you never can be sure."

"Bet"

Ron and his two mans got their shit and

rolled out. The meet was about fifteen minutes from the spot...

As the team rolled up to Dev and Los they explained on what was gonna happen
        and they all rolled up and turned the cars the opposite direction. Everyone got in their positions and we waited to see Two-Tone and the rest of them position around the crib. I was the first to start throwing the grenades. Me and Twan threw ours and seen Smooth, James, and Sid throw theirs. After a second it was on. Shit started explodin and all you heard was screams. One nigga came out the front and Sid dropped him with four shots in the chest. We all rushed in the crib. There were about six bodies on the floor, two niggas were scramblin up the steps I shot one nigga in his back and he fell over the rail. Smooth ran up the steps spittin his HK. I mean shit was coming along smoothly then there was a loud "BANG". I looked and Sid fell next to me. I looked and seen this nigga "E" at the top of the steps bussin an AK of his own. Smooth was trying to hit him but was missin. "E" dipped back and threw something. Smooth started up the steps

and was hit like six times, then fell on the steps and then there was an explosion that threw him over the rail. I started to become noid because this nigga was half ass serious. I got up and hurried to the kitchen soon as I opened the door a knife came flying pass my face. I only could respond by shooting that bitch in the chest. Twan was in the dining room holding his until an explosion sent his left leg and arm flying, the shrapnal also hit James but he was able to drop the two that was behind the wall with a green bandit of his own. Rell and his team had better luck. After they dropped their grenades they rushed into the basement and there were about two dead one was crawling up the steps. Reese rushed the steps and put one in his head. Soon as he ended that niggas life he looked up into a barrel of a pump. Ant shot that nigga in the face which in turn made him fire the pump, which flipped Reese backwards down the steps. Buck checked around the corners and then they ran up the steps. Soon as they cleared the kitchen and meeting up with Crock they went to the living room. The room looked empty and we began to spread out then we seen a nigga slide over and started bussin at us and I tried to dive outa the way and was hit in the shoulder. Two-Tone was shootin it out with him and drooped him but not before taking a shot to his right hand. James was up stairs looking fot that nigga "E". he was low and had his hammer at the ready. He seen that nighga runnin around but tried his best to stay calm. He followed that nigga into a room and then was shocked to see that the room was empty. I mean no furniture or doors he then knew he was spun. He turned around and that nigga was standing there with his gun at his face.

"Drop it" James did as he was told "E" continued with, "Have you prayed to your maker?" "E" asked James seen Ant coming up the steps and tried to buy time.

"You got some suggestions" James said Confused by the comment he stalled long enough Ant signaled him to dive away and James did so. Ant shot "E" threee times in the back and walked up and kicked his gun away.ant looked in his

face and said,
"Look at you now nigga, I can't hear you what you say D, D, D, D, D, D, Dipset? I hate to tell you but your whole sets just been dipped. You bitch ass nigga." Ant finished his statement with two shots in that niggas face. James got up and put his fist out for some dap.
"You my nigga, you just saved my ass nigga I owe you."
"Nah we family you'd do the same thing."
"True Dat"

After the house was secure they all got together in the front of the building. I seen James come out and asked,
"You aight nigga?" and pointed to a cut on his neck
"Yeah I'ma make it."
"How is everyong?" Devin asked counting everyone in attendance.
"We aight" Rell and Buck answered together
"I'll live "Two-Tone said
"Look roght, everyone go home and get cleaned up. If yall seen something yall liked better go get it cause I'm burnin this bitch down."
"That nigga aint have shit in there, burn

that shit." Rell said
Everyone left and went in there own directions...

Black, Ron and D-Nice all walked into the spot and waited a minute until they came. Tori walked into the spot with four niggas as she said. Two of them stood by the doors and the other two posted themselves behind Tori. Ron had a glock .17 in his holster and a heavy sweat shirt to help conceal it. He also had a .45 sitting inside the briefcase under some money knowing she wont rummage through the back bills. Black and D-Nice stood there ready to handle them niggas behind her. Black was trying to hold back from hittin her now because he knew the ime would come as long as he listened to Ron.

"I hear you wanna do some business?" Tori said with her familiar accent. Sitting down now but she had a tight ass body; she was in a suit with somw pumps and had her hair in a bun.

"Yeah me and my team wanna move up with the big fish." Ron replied

"Well you come to the right person, what you lookin to spend?" she asked

Ron was careful when he opened the case and showed her fourty grand

"I got one hundred and twenty grand in each case so let me know."

Black and D-nice were still trained on the guards and didn't move.

"I like that she said and snapped her fingers, the two men at the door turned and left the room. Ron turned the case around and shuffled for the gunas inconspicous as possible and found it. He knew this was his chance.

"A, you hear about them crazy ass P.D.K. niggas fallin off?"

Hearing this Black and D-Nice knew what time it was.

"Yeah they had what I like to call too much pride. They fell like flies, too bad though they had a real empire which just crumbled. Maybe lack of leadership."

"Damn I almost forgot my boss told me to tell you something." Before she had the chance to respond Ron stood with his .45 and shot her twice in the face which blew her bun off the back of her head. The guards came to the door and dropped the bags and tried to pull out their hammers. Ron shot one of them twice in the chest and he fell. The other one dipped behind a wall. Black and D-Nice were on some desperado shit. They dropped the cases revealing their hellafied killing systems (HKS) and started to spit at the two they been eyeing. Ron reached for his and heard a loud BOOM!! Then everything seemed quiet. he pulled the case up and was closing it when he noticed the money had red stains on it that looked fresh. He closed the case and seen more blood drops fall on the case. He felt a tingling sensation behind his left ear. As he reached he felt a hole behind his ear and seen he was shot. He looked at Black and seen him saying something cause his lips were moving but Ron heard nothing. He carried the case and everything went blank. Black rushed over and grabbed the money and rolled with D-Nice. As hurt as he was they knew they had to leave, they would tell Rell in the morning if they had time...

Chapter 16

About a week went by and Rell has been trying to adjust to not worrying about that nigga from D.C. He was still a bit cautious on what to do about them niggas from Wes. V. soon as he thought abput that his phone rang.

"Yo"

"Rell we lost Ron!" D-Nice said with a bit of a sob.

"Lost him what you talkin about nigga?"

"We handled the problem from Wes. V. and he slipped up."

"Damn you and Black cool?"

"Yeah we cool but we gonna fall back for a while." responded D-Nice.

"Yeah that's good."

"A I'll holla at you on the rebound."

"Aight"

Rell was drivin to the spot on frankford to see if anyone wanted to handle some work. He knew there was a young nigga named Taz who was on his top. So he went to holla at.

"Taz"

"Yo what's up Rell, what you doing around here?"

"Tryin to see if you want a job"

"Yeah nigga what I gotta do?"

"Find youself some loyal niggas to ride with you and start selling this shit the prices are on the bag."

"Aight"

Rell handed him the bag and rolled out. Rell turned on the first corner and was pulled over. He thought to himself that this must be a bullshit jawn. The officer pulled his glock out and ordered him to step out of the vehicle. Rell got out and did as he was told.

"Step to the back of the vehicle and keep your hands where I can see them."

"Drop down to your knees and lay face down on the ground." Soon as he did he was cuffed and detained...

Buck was at the strip with Ant, James and Two-Tone bussin it up about the lasting memory of "E".

"That nigga wasn't sweet I thought I was done." James said

"Yeah yopur face was blank like you was on some fuckit shit." Ant said

"Nah that nigga shit his pants when he seen that barrel." Two-Tone joked

'Fuck outta here nigga you was hiding in

the stove duckin bullets." James cut at
him. They all had their fun. Buck was
laughing when his phone rang.
"Hold on yall he answered, "Hello"
"You have a collect call from "Ant" at the
beep buck hit one soon as he heard the
name.
'Yo nigga what the fuck?" buck said
"This shit crazy dog they got me booked
and they tryin to roof me."
"What's the charge?"
"Conspiracy, with multiple counts of drug
trafficing, and multiple counts of
homicide. Plus they say they got a
witness to the murders of Boo and Lynx
from a year ago."
"Damn nigga I'll call you a lawyer."
"I handled that already just see if you can
get some change for bail.
"What is it?"
"One mil straight."
"Damn nigga that's goin into the stash."
"I gotta go but see what you can do."
"Aight" Buck hung up and called Crock.
But got no answer.
"I gotta go yall I'll holla in a minute."
"Aight" they said as they were still joking
with each other. Buck felt that with Rell

out the way he would become the next thing to Crock. If Crock was to slip then he would run the empire. Buck went to holla t Two-Tone and Dumas. They had their packs on tiome as usual and Buck made sure they were re-uped. Buck was ridin around havin a good time crackin on bitches at stop lights and even got a couple numbers. After he was done collecting he went home to his girl, where he planned to eat and get some sleep...

After sleeping damn near the whole day away, I went to see my girl who was beginning to show. She was horny as hell but said she wanted to wait another week to have sex but she'd go down. I could careless how I got my nut off but she was on some cautious shit. Whe we finished she cooked some dinner for a nigga. I was planning on staying with her for a while just to stay outa the way for a minute. Then my cell buzzed.

"Yo" I answered

"Crock! What the fuck nigga" Rell yelled through the phone

"What the fuck is wrong with you?"

"What you mean what's wrong with me you know where I'm at?"

"Nah why am I suppose to know?"
"Yeah mother fucka. I'm in jail nigga.
Buck aint tell you?" he asked
"Buck aint tell me shit, I aint even been
out my girl crib today and you the first
person who called."
"That nigga's a fuckin Bitch, look man I'm
done nigga."
"Done what you mean done?"
"They got witnesses and motherfuckas
testifying about some niggas I killed, and
them seeing me drive drugs across state
and all this other shit."
"You don't know them?" I asked
concerned for my own freedom.
"Nah, try to send some change to hold me
down."
"Aight I'ma hit an all night check cashing
spot later."
"Aight be safe nigga."
"Bet that!"
     I hung up and told Meme I had to
handle something real quick. I gave her a
hug and kissed her belly and rolled out.
"Hurry back" she yelled
"I'll try!"
     I left to the crib and opened my safe
in the basement. The only other person

who knew of it was Meme and the combo was my b-day. I had grabbed like two grand and put it in a check to him and mailed it out. I went back to my crib and seen the block was packed. I was gone maybe twenty minutes and that shit gets packed. I found a parking space at the corner of the block. I got out and seen this nigga Lester who was watching the spot for me. I called him.

"Yo! Lester" as I did I felt an eery sense of De `ja vu. As he was walking up he said, "A Crock how's the wifey and the youngin?"

"We aight you aint seen Rell did you?"

"Nah I'll tell him you wanted to see him."

"Aight"

I turned up the street and seen this nigga running down the street calling Lester. He got up about a door or two away from me I stepped aside to let him pass. He Stopped next to me and asked "A homie you got the time?" With a real familiar voice. Paying it no mind I looked at my watch.

"Yeah ten thirty man." I couldn't help but think this shit happened before. I started to look up and this nigga pulled a gun from his coat.

BOOM!! BOOM!! BOOM!!

I fell back and stumbled onto the car and this nigga hit me again. BOOM!!

I felt the first three shots but the fourth I couldn't feel. I fell to the ground and layed there looking at the stars. I started thinking I do remember. That wasn't a dream that was a warning that I paid no attention to. I started to chuckle a bit cause it was funny to me. This nigga stood over me and pointed his gun at my chest. I seen his face and recognized him immediately as Onnie. "What this nigga caught me slippin like that?" I said to my self. I knew better than this. He caught me on some ol Benny Blanco shit. He started saying

"Yeah! What you gonna do now nigga? Pay back aint it a bitch? Die slow mother fucka!" BOOM!! BOOM!! He ran off, as I felt my life slip I started tremblin cause it got cold. I couldn't hear or feel my heart beating any more. I closed my eyes and said to myself.

"Every dollar made a struggle. I went through mad struggles to become a made man... look at me now!!"

Conclusion

Rell was found guilty on the following charges, Drug possession with the intent to sell, Drug trafficking, weapons possession, multiple homicides, and the possession of a fully automatic firearm. He was sentenced to three consecutive life terms and 210 days running concurrent...

Devin and Oscar started moving their own shit out there in D.C. since they have been there so long people already recognized them and respected them even more. There shits been poppin for the last six months and now they have their own empire. They built their own mansion and put up a couple clubs, they been doing their damn thing...

Buck has taken over the P.D.K. empire since the death of Crock and incarceration of Rell. He had them niggas movin heavy. He eventually took one in the head from some low rank nigga on his team. Ant has been running the empire and been killing the game...

Meme has been living off of the money that Crock had been putting in the safe in the basement. She counted it one day and found out it was over ten million. She distributed three bonds of one million to the families of Rell, Buck, and Blaze. She never thought it was that much money in a small safe. She had her son and named him Dave after his father. She tells him constantly his father died while protecting his family...

This has been a story by David Austin

Epilogue

Throughout life people never realize how precious the human life is, until it's **their** life which is draining. To all beginnings there must come an end and this is the last struggle that Crock and the majority of P.D.K. will experience on their road to becoming made men. I hope you've enjoyed these novels, and please take them as a learning experience and not a tutorial. Wouldn't want to read your story in the obituary section of the news papers...

David A.
A.K.A. Crock

www.ingramcontent.com/pod-product-compliance
Lightning Source LLC
Chambersburg PA
CBHW020624250626
47154CB00004B/1663